Wrong

BREAKING THE RULES SERIES
BOOK TWO

Mandy,
XOXO

K Webster

K. Webster

Dedication

To my angels—I may have done a lot of things the "wrong" way, but with you two, I'd say I did it perfectly right. Mommy loves you.

Prologue

Pepper

Senior Year

"**PSST…**" a male voice whispered to me, dragging my attention from the calculus teacher. My eyes met none other than Cole Stine. He was absolutely gorgeous, and I spent a lot of days daydreaming about him.

Why is he talking to me again? This was the fourth time he'd talked to me this week—actually acknowledged that I existed. This was Cole Stine, of course I was counting!

"What?" I asked, leaning towards him. I could smell his cologne, and my heart raced. Guys like Cole didn't usually talk to me. *Ever.* This week was a first.

"What grade do you have in here?" he whispered back to me.

"A ninety-eight."

"That's what I thought. I'll pay you to tutor me. My football scholarship rides on me passing this class."

I nodded because I didn't know what else to do. Each time he'd talked to me, it was to tell me a joke or to ask if I liked a certain band. Those four brief conversations had been replayed over and over again in my mind—every word and smile he offered had been seared pleasurably into my memory. When he grinned at me, bringing me back from my daydreaming, I melted. Freaking-hot

Cole wanted me to tutor him which would be one on one alone time. *Um, yes please.* I smiled, which I didn't do much of in that awful school, and returned my attention back to the teacher.

Once class ended, he came over and sat on the edge of my desk as I was putting away my books in my bag. I smelled him again and had to force my hands not to shake. He made me nervous but in a good way.

"Write down your address and phone number. I'll come over this afternoon if that's okay and bring the Halestorm album I was telling you about to listen to while we study. You can borrow it and let me know what you think." He winked at me which made breathing really hard. It was difficult not to hyperventilate in his presence. *Could this mean that we could be friends?*

I nodded again, at a loss for words, and scrambled for a piece of paper. He handed me a pen and held his arm to me. *Oh my God.* He wanted me to write on him. I was seriously freaking out right now.

Tentatively, I put my fingers around his wrist and drew him closer to me. I wanted to drag on this moment, but if I wrote any slower, he'd know I was being a total creeper. When I finished and looked up at him, he was grinning at me again. My face blushed from embarrassment. Laughing, he hopped off my desk and waved goodbye. Cole *freaking-hot* Stine was coming to my house today.

The knock on the front door made me jump, and I raced to open it. The idea of having the hottest guy at school in my house was making me crazy with excitement. School had been hard for me socially. I was shy and didn't make friends very easily. Most of the girls ignored me and the guys definitely didn't notice me. I couldn't wait to start college in the fall and begin a fresh new life.

Maybe I'd actually make a friend or two.

I opened the door and my breath caught. Cole was so gorgeous. His black hair was spiked in all different directions. The muscles in his shoulders and arms made him look way too big to be in high school. He'd definitely kill it in college football. Icy blue eyes caught me in their gaze.

"Can I come in?" he asked, smiling.

Motioning him in, I led him to the living room, where I had my books spread across the coffee table. "Would you like a drink?" I offered as he sat on the sofa.

He shook his head, so I sat beside him. Trying to get past the awkwardness of having *the* hot Cole Stine in my living room, I jumped right into the tutoring. He seemed to be listening at first but then proceeded to just stare at me.

"I've noticed you for a long time. You're very pretty, you know," he admitted.

My heart pounded at his words. *Me? Pretty?*

"I, uh, thanks," I stammered, unsure how to respond properly. Warmth flooded my neck and cheeks. I hoped he wouldn't realize how embarrassed I was at the moment.

My mom poked her head in, thankfully distracting me from his intense gaze and my social ineptitude. "Honey, I need to run to the store. Are you sure you'll be okay just the two of you?"

She knew how few friends I had and how socially awkward I could be. I nodded at her and she waved, leaving us alone in the house. Nervously, I popped a piece of peppermint gum into my mouth to distract me from my proximity to Cole. Trying to focus on our lesson, I pointed back to the calculus book to show him something that needed noting. His hand darted out and captured mine.

My eyes jerked to his, because there was no way Cole Stine could ever like a girl like me. He was smiling at me, and his look was full of heat. I squirmed a little because I'd never kissed anyone before, and he was looking at my lips like he wanted to devour them. When I started to say something, he took his other hand and lifted my chin up.

"I want to kiss you," he uttered softly, reluctantly dragging his eyes from my lips.

"Okay," I breathed out.

His grin was almost my undoing. Dipping forward, he grazed his lips across mine, causing me to shiver. I could not believe this was happening.

I parted my lips, and he gently pressed his to mine. My heart was beating wildly in my chest. When his tongue slipped into my mouth, I moaned softly because this was perfect. My first kiss was flawless. His hands threaded through my hair as he deepened the kiss. He laughed once he realized that he'd stolen my gum. I was tingling all over because this was quite possibly the best moment in my life.

As if a flip had switched, our kisses became hungry and needy. His hands were all over my body, and I let them since it felt good. When his large hand slipped up my shirt, I gasped. I didn't really want to go there, but I didn't want to stop him either. He gently laid me backwards, still kissing me furiously. His hand eased up to my breast and I moaned again when he touched it.

He growled into my mouth as he lay over me to get closer. I could feel his hardness through his jeans pressing against my own sensitive area and it made me jump. His kisses became more hurried as he pushed himself hard against me. The hand that was on my breast started to roughly grab me now. I suddenly pulled my mind out of the passionate moment and wrenched my mouth from his.

"Cole, we need to stop."

He ignored me and kissed me again, more insistent, as he

pressed into me between my legs.

Pushing against his chest, I firmly told him, "Cole! I said stop. Get off of me."

When he slightly lifted away from me, he was glaring. "Are you being a fucking tease? I'll have blue balls if I don't come. At least jerk me off," he spat. His sudden change of demeanor chilled me to the bone.

"No! This is wrong. Get off of me, Cole. I'm done. You need to leave," I begged as tears fill my eyes. I felt trapped underneath his heavy body that was making no moves to get up.

Without another word, he fumbled for the top of my yoga pants and started to wrench them down my body. I screamed and thrashed against him, but he was too strong. His hand covered my mouth, and I whimpered from underneath him.

I started really squirming and wiggling when he reached down to undo his jeans. Managing to get them down far enough to pull out his penis, he tried to hold me still so he could force it in but since my pants weren't all the way off, he was having difficulty. I sobbed loudly as I prepared myself for what was about to happen.

When we heard the footsteps across the hardwood floor in the living room, he froze, which thankfully stopped him from taking what wasn't his—my virginity. I was crying and still squirming, trying to get away, when he was ripped forcefully from me. Daddy was towering above me with his hand gripped tightly around Cole's throat. Thank God he didn't have to stay late at the office today and was right on time coming home from work.

"Daddy!" I screamed as I frantically pulled my pants up and scrambled off of the couch, doing my best to put distance between me and Cole.

Cole's face was turning bright red as he tried to free his neck from Daddy's hand. Daddy finally let go and shoved him away.

"Get the hell out of my house, you little worm! Don't you ever so much as look at my daughter again or I will choke the life out of you!" I'd never seen Daddy so furious in my life.

Cole bolted towards the front door, yanking his pants up along the way. I was wailing still, and Daddy ran over to me, wrapping his protective arms around me. "My princess. Everything's going to be okay. Daddy's here now." He held my trembling body until my sobbing subsided.

Apparently the cops couldn't do anything. It was our word against his. There was no physical evidence because he hadn't made it that far. So Daddy sent Cole's family a very strongly worded legal letter that threatened his future if he ever messed with me again. After several days of missing school, I finally had to face going back.

When I walked into the school, all eyes were on me.

What the hell is everyone staring at?

Their whispers made me feel sick to my stomach.

Did Cole tell everyone what happened?

"She accused him of trying to rape her. Cole Stine would never even so much as look as her, much less sleep with her," a voice whispered beside me as I walked past. I flinched at his words.

"Peppermint Pussy. That's her new name. He said when she threw herself at him, she smelled like peppermint. I can smell her from here."

Tears filled my eyes as I walked to my locker. These people were unreal. He had forced himself on me, but because I was a nobody, he was the victim.

Day after day for nearly a week, I suffered humiliation from those idiots. At first, I was devastated and nearly feigned illness so I wouldn't have to come back. Each day, Cole would sit in his seat beside me. His smug attitude suffocated me in the classroom but I chose to ignore his presence.

Today, when the people in the halls began their chanting, "Peppermint Pussy," my blood began to boil. Cole was a monster and these people were supporting him. Ignoring them all like I had done every day, I stomped into my calculus class and dropped into my seat, refusing to look at any of them.

When his familiar cologne invaded my senses, I felt like puking. He leaned towards me, and I shuddered at his proximity. This was his first attempt at making contact with me since the incident. The hairs on my neck stood up when he spoke.

"It's a good thing I didn't get to fuck you. My dick would have frozen and fallen off. I hear your Peppermint Pussy is wicked," he spat at me.

Having finally had enough, I furiously jerked my head towards him. I was my Daddy's girl, which meant that I would no longer allow him to intimidate me. He was glaring at me menacingly, and I tried not to flinch. Memories of the other day flooded my mind but I forced them away. Instead, I held my chin up and faced him.

Glaring at him with hate filled eyes, I spoke evenly when I said, "You say one more thing about me and I'll have my dad nail your ass to the wall. He's an attorney, and the only reason he hasn't pursued ruining your life is because I begged him not to. I just wanted to forget that it ever happened. But your dumb ass won't let me forget, which means I'm going to have him make sure that your life is over. You'll never play football in college when I'm done with you."

His eyes narrowed as he took in what I'd had to say. I could see that his brain was working out whether or not I had been telling the truth.

When I leaned forward a little more, trying not to choke on his scent, I whispered, "He will ruin you."

"Bitch," he muttered under his breath but turned and opened his book. I took that as his surrender and I opened my own book. My heart pounded furiously to what I considered my victory. The corners of my lips curled up in a smile—the first one since before he set out to terrorize me. If feeling awesome for what I'd just done made me a bitch, then I definitely loved being one.

Chapter ONE

Pepper

I SIPPED MY WINE as I listened to Andi groan about her first day at work. We were sitting comfortably in a booth at the back of Dempsey's bar. Andi always got herself in the weirdest predicaments. Her weekend beau, who was the biggest asshole ever, was now one of her bosses. And to top it all off, he'd treated her like dirt today, as if the weekend had meant nothing. I hoped that was the end of her stupid little game she liked to play. She was still a fragile girl, and I hated that she had to sleep around to act human.

The alternative was unacceptable though. Those weeks leading to her accidental overdose had been pure hell for the both of us. If the pills hadn't almost killed her, malnutrition would have. She was a shell of herself, and I'd died a little every day from having to see her that way.

Andi was my best friend. From the moment she bounded into the dorm room four and a half years ago, blond hair bouncing in her ponytail, I had been instantly drawn to her. She'd looked like the typical snotty bitch like I was used to dealing with from my high school—until she smiled. When Andi smiled, she lit up the room.

I'd tried to avoid her at first, unsure of how to be a normal social being, especially after what had happened with Cole. Quite honestly, I'd wanted to put up walls and not talk to anyone. But with Andi, it had been impossible because she had been like a cute little puppy that wouldn't go away.

That first day, she stuck out her hand to me. "I'm Andi, short for Miranda. I'm from Indiana." She beamed at me, and my heart craved the possibility of a friendship with someone who didn't know my past. I could be anyone I wanted to be now that I was in college. There was no room in my life anymore for the shy, scared girl I used to be.

Shaking her hand, I just said, "Pepper." What could I say? If we were going for alter egos here…

"Pepper? Like salt and pepper?" she asked quizzically.

"The one and only," I grumbled, trying not to smile at her but failing miserably.

Once she decided that I wasn't messing with her, she threw her arms around me and hugged my neck. My heart thudded to life at the prospect of having a real friend. Andi seemed like a genuine person.

I snapped back to present time when she grabbed my hand. "Shit, Pepper. They're here. Jordan and Jackson are here. We should go."

Of course I swiveled my head to where she was looking so I could give Jackson the evil eye. *Bastard.* I was a little distracted when my eyes skirted over to his brother, Jordan. He looked quite different than his bastard brother. His hair was brown, but not as dark as Jackson's. It was styled a little messier than his brother's was. When his green eyes met mine, my stomach did a flip-flop. *What the hell?* Jordan grinned at us with a goofy smile and sauntered over to us.

"Andi! Surprise seeing you here. Let me buy you and your lovely friend here a drink." His eyes fell to mine when he said 'lovely,' and I felt exposed under his gaze. Andi looked horrified, so I figured this was our cue to leave.

"We were about to leave," I told him icily as I began scooting from the booth.

"Nonsense!" he boomed and sat down beside me, bumping me back into the booth with his hip. He started barking out orders to the bartender. Jackson finally made it over to the table and sat far from Andi. She looked like she wanted to puke.

Jordan's thigh touching my own sent a spark of electricity through me and I shuddered, not used to being affected like this. He turned to me and grinned again. I thought they called those "panty-melting grins." Mine were definitely on fire right now.

His eyes studied my face, probably taking in my glasses, lack of makeup, and messy bun. I didn't care though. This was who I was. He turned and said something to Andi about Jackson but I ignored him, taking a moment to compose myself. He made me feel weak, like my former self from high school, and it made me sick. No man would make me feel weak again. I was Pepper the Bitch. Something about him affected me though, and I hated the feeling.

"Andi here was just telling me about her wonderful day at work," I said sarcastically as I glared at Jackson, who was avoiding everyone's gaze.

"Great! I'm so glad, Andi. I think you'll really like it there. Everyone works hard to make it a successfully company," he told us as our drinks arrived. Under his breath, he muttered to me, "I feared Jackson might have scared her off like he does everyone else. He's an asshole." I laughed in agreement.

Andi and Jackson were having a silent standoff from across the table. Jordan was completely oblivious as he told some funny stories of him and his brother.

"So, Pepper, what do you do for a living?" he asked, genuinely interested. Here's the part where the guy's eyes would glaze over.

"I'm an assistant production manager at the Metropolitan Museum of Art. Mostly I handle our annual pledges from our donors, events, and overall success of the museum. The production manager, Stan, basically gives me all of his grunt work, but it is an awesome experience." I waited for the subject change because it always came about now.

"So do you get to help with any of the exhibits?" he questioned.

My eyes darted to his. *Why is he inquiring about my job?* We were supposed to be moving on to topics like the weather or sports or some shit.

"Um, well, yes, if they center around an event," I told him hesitantly, still waiting for him to lose interest. I was one of the very few people I knew who was actually interested in this sort of thing.

"So did you get to help any with the Silla? Those ancient treasures from the Korean kingdom so many years ago are absolutely fascinating. I took my mother to see it a few weeks ago."

My jaw dropped. He knew about the Silla?

"Yes. I, uh, helped make sure everything went smoothly and that it is being promoted properly to draw in the crowds we were expecting. It will be one of the highlights at the upcoming gala."

"What gala? Do you need any sponsors?" he asked.

"No, the sponsorships are filled and have been for some time. It's our annual gala that brings in quite a few hefty donations that get us through the next year. I've been working my tail off to make sure it goes off without a hitch."

"Do you need a date for the gala?" he asked, eyebrow raised cockily. *Subject officially changed.* It had only been a matter of time.

"No. I won't have time for that sort of thing. I'll be working the event, so there'll be no time for socializing."

"Let me take you out another night then. Tomorrow night?"

Man, this guy was ballsy. I couldn't stand his brother, and he was my best friend's boss. Not touching that with a ten-foot pole.

My eyes flitted over to Andi, who was chugging her wine while Jackson undressed her with his eyes. He then stood quickly and excused himself for the evening. Good, I was tired of looking at him.

"No, Jordan, I am going to have to decline your offer. I'm busy. Come on, Andi. I have an early morning tomorrow so we should go."

She nodded and excused herself to the bathroom. Jordan stared at me for a moment, his eyes searching my own. It appeared that he didn't get turned down often because I could tell that his mind was working as he tried to figure out why.

I nudged him with my knee, indicating that I wanted out of the booth. The shock wore off and he chuckled, scooting out. When I got to the edge, he offered his hand and helped me from the booth. His hand was large and hard, which made a shiver run through my body. Yep, he totally made me feel weak. Not too nicely, I yanked my hand from his and stalked over to Andi, leaving him to stare after us.

Chapter TWO

Jordan

PEPPER WAS QUITE the firecracker. She was evidently the only woman alive immune to my charms. I was completely intrigued with her. Typically, I dated girls who flaunted their beauty. And Pepper, even though she didn't flaunt it whatsoever, was indeed beautiful.

Her brown eyes flared with fire whenever she spoke. The words coming out of her mouth might have been frosty, but the light behind her eyes made me believe there was an intensity that she tried hard to suppress.

Her glasses just made her look adorable. And her messy bun on top of her head completed the sexy librarian look. The baggy college sweatshirt she was wearing could hardly hide her curves. My eyes appreciated the swell of her ass through her jeans as she left the bar arm in arm with Andi. She looked like the type who could be a freak beneath the sheets. And dammit, I wanted to find out if it was true.

Heading out to my car that was parked in front of the bar, I pulled out my cell to call Jackson.

"What the hell, man?" I asked once he answered.

He just grunted into the phone. The whole thing with Nadia

really made him a bear to be around. She was a cheater in more ways than one. I wouldn't be the only one sighing in relief when their divorce was finalized. It didn't stop me from harassing him though.

"You seriously just got up and left in the middle of our conversation. What kind of douche leaves two hot ladies so he can go home and sleep? Come on, man. That was just lame. I can see you and Andi have the hots for each other. I'd hit that if I were you," I teased, laughing, trying to get a rise out of him.

"You aren't me," he growled into the phone. *Testy.* I guessed that he must like her because if that wasn't his way of staking his claim, I didn't know what else it could be.

"Whatever, dude. I'll see you tomorrow. Don't forget. The new guy, Brayden Greene, starts tomorrow. It would be nice if you could get to work on time. And try to be nicer to Andi tomorrow. I hate it when you make my assistants cry."

When Andi walked in, I smiled at her. My eyes darted to her legs because her skirt was so damn short. I grinned at her, knowing that my brother was going to have a fit. She was trying to drive him crazy with that outfit and it was definitely going to work.

Jackson looked like he wanted to pounce on her, but when the new guy jumped up to hug her and held on a little too long, I thought Jackson was going to kill him.

The poor girl looked like she was going to die under Jackson's intense gaze, so I patted her knee for comfort when she sat beside me. The rest of the meeting went on without any more issues.

After everyone went their separate ways, I sat in my office thinking about Pepper again. She was so damn enigmatic and it drove me nuts. I thought she'd acted like she might have a mutual

attraction for me, but she'd quickly hid it away. If only I could figure out a way to get the main sponsor dumped. Then she'd have to
see me.

Late that afternoon, I thought I would see if Andi could use
her pull as Pepper's best friend to help me out. Trying to seem
nonchalant, I stepped out of my office and strode over to her desk.

"Andi, I need a favor. The firm is really needing some good
publicity. The museum where your friend Pepper works is having a
gala event soon. They've already pinned down their sponsors, but I
want Compton Enterprises to be the main sponsor. I don't care
how much it costs and how much persuading it takes, but please
make it happen," I authoritatively instructed. She nodded in
agreement so I turned on my heels and made my way back to my
desk.

After a brief search on the computer, I brought up the website
to see just who my competition was going to be for the gala sponsorship. I laughed out loud when I realized that the main sponsor
was a good buddy of mine. Picking up the phone, I gave him a call.

"Trent, how are things in the financial world?" I asked when
he answered.

"Jordan! Things are great. What about you and Jackson? How
is everything going lately? Have you determined any more about
those shady business deals?" he asked.

Trent had been a good friend to us during those hard days after
my dad passed away. He'd looked over all of the financials with us
and made some suggestions so that we could remain on the right
track. I trusted him with my life.

Now that the shit had hit the fan with this one particular business deal Dad had made, Trent was helping us determine our op-
tions. We'd just had a meeting last Saturday to iron out some
plans.

"Things are great, man. Listen, I need a really huge favor. It's going to sound crazy, but I've done crazier shit in my life." He laughed because, being a frat brother, he knew most of that crazy shit I'd done.

"Go on, man. What is it?"

"I just discovered that Sutton Investments is the main sponsor for the Metropolitan Museum of Art's annual gala."

"And?" he questioned, unsure where I was going with this.

"I need you to pull out. There's this girl," I began, and he burst out laughing on the other line.

"You do realize the sponsorship is for half a million dollars?"

"Yes, and I even plan to make a donation to sweeten the deal. I want this girl—bad. She won't give me the time of day. If I step in as main sponsor, she'll have no excuse not to see me."

Trent was laughing hysterically on the other line again, but he finally grew quiet.

"Listen, Jordan. I know your financial situation. Do you really think it's a good idea to pour your excess cash flow into something like this for a woman?"

"Trent, we'll just take the money from my trust, not the company. I won't jeopardize Compton Enterprises like that. But I really want this. I'll owe you big time. Name your price, man."

He silently contemplated his decision.

"Okay, I'll call Stan right now and pull out, but under one condition," he said, going in for the kill.

"I said name your price, dude. Anything. No joke."

"I get your Super Bowl tickets this year."

Shit. "Done. This is why you're one of my best friends."

Hanging up the phone, I smiled. Pepper was by far the most work I'd ever put forth to pursue a woman. For some reason, I knew she'd be worth it.

When Andi burst into my office a couple of hours later, I knew that Trent had pulled through and he was going to have fun at the Super Bowl this year.

"Pepper just texted me saying that their main sponsor pulled out for the gala. Here's her business card. Call her and set it up. I bet she'll be happy to find a quick replacement," she gushed, excitedly thrusting Pepper's card at me. Andi was on Team Jordan.

I picked up the phone, dialing Pepper's number as Andi left.

"Pepper Jones speaking," she huffed into the phone. Oh, she was pissed all right.

"Pepper, hi...it's me, Jordan Compton. I hear your main sponsor pulled out. Compton Enterprises would love to take their place as main sponsor."

She was quiet for a moment before she popped her gum loudly into the phone.

"There's a list of people who are before you who have first right of refusal to the sponsorship. I'll let you know."

She hung up on me and I laughed. That girl was going to make me fucking chase her and I was going to enjoy every minute of it.

Chapter THREE

Pepper

I STILL COULDN'T BELIEVE that Sutton Investments had pulled out less than two weeks away from the gala. Stan was all over my ass to find a new sponsor because obviously he would be the one feeling the heat if we couldn't find a replacement. I'd only been there for five months and I really didn't want this one thing to define the rest of my career.

After Andi had come in this evening, explaining to me her hand in telling Jordan about the sponsorship opening, I had been furious. I'd spent the rest of the night calling and emailing other possible companies. Unfortunately, this late in the year, they'd already all made other commitments. As much as I hated the idea, I was going to have to give in to Jordan's offer.

The next morning, I called Jordan at eight on the dot.

"This is Jordan," he spoke smoothly, sounding annoyingly sure of himself.

"Hi, it's me, Pepper Jones. Uh, I was going to let you know that you can have the main sponsorship if you still want it. What we'll need now is—" I said but was cut off when he interrupted.

"Of course we want the sponsorship. We'll discuss it over dinner tonight. I'll pick you up from the museum just after five."

"Wait, what? No."

"Pepper, I have a few requests and I think we should discuss them further."

"No, absolutely not. I know what you're doing here, Jordan," I snapped.

"What? We both have to eat and we have business to discuss."

He was trying to play innocent, but I knew exactly what he was doing.

"Jordan, this isn't a good—"

"I have a sizeable donation I'd like to make to the museum but if you're not interested, I understand."

I knew he was baiting me. But, considering my career was riding on this deal, I needed to change my tone—and quick.

"No, no! I'm sorry, er, yes, we would love to have your donation," I finally conceded through clenched teeth.

"Good, it's been decided. See you soon."

Click.

I was going to tell him I would just meet up with him at the restaurant but he had already hung up on me. The fucker *hung* up on me!

My blood boiled as I thought about how this pompous ass had injected himself into my life. Every time I thought about his handsome face grinning at me, I wanted to throw my laptop against the wall.

When a knock sounded on the door, I took a deep breath, pushing out my anger as I exhaled. I looked up to see Stan watching me.

"Did you find a replacement yet, Pepper?" he asked with his arms crossed. Stan was a pretty good-looking guy. He might have even been my type had I actually had one. His dark curly hair was cropped short on his head, but it would start to curl around his ears if he went too long without a haircut. I glanced down at his dress shirt that stretched over his muscled chest and biceps. He really should have bought bigger shirts. It was distracting.

Dragging my eyes back to his, I said, "Yeah, Compton Enterprises. They want to add a 'sizeable' donation as well. Mr. Compton and I are going to dinner tonight to discuss it all in further detail."

His eyes darkened as he looked me over.

"That's nonsense. I'll be going to dinner with him. I need to make sure the sponsorship is finalized and that I can get as much as I can from the donation. Where are you supposed to be meeting him?"

My mouth dropped open. He seriously thought I was incapable of handling things with Jordan. Standing up, I stalked over to him with my finger in his face.

"He's picking me up at five. Stan, I can handle it. You can't just take over like this! Trust me."

Swatting my hand out of his face, he stormed out of the office, but not before saying, "I can and will do this. Watch me. And if you know what's good for you, you won't yell at your boss."

For the rest of the day, I stewed with anger. At first, I had been miffed at having to go to dinner with Jordan. But now that I had been told that I couldn't, it was all I wanted to do. Damn, I was a stubborn woman.

I finally looked up from my laptop hours later when someone knocked on my door. Jordan's handsome face was grinning at me. My heart fluttered on its own accord. The smile that popped up automatically across my face pissed me off. My body had its own ideas that my mind didn't necessarily agree with whenever Jordan was around.

"Jordan, nice to see you," I greeted formally, standing to go over and shake his hand.

He willingly took my hand in his and held on to it.

"Um, it looks like there is a slight change of plans," I huffed out, frowning. It was embarrassing that I'd been trumped by my boss.

His smile fell but he didn't release my hand and it sent chills up my arm.

"What do you mean?"

"Well, my boss, Stan, wants to go to dinner with you to talk about the sponsorship. So it looks like I'm out." I couldn't help it when my chin quivered for just a moment. Biting my lip, I stopped it from continuing. His scowl let me know that he saw that I was upset by this new revelation.

"No." One simple word, but my heart pounded when he spoke it.

"Jordan, there's nothing I can do about it. He's my boss. I have to do what he says." His eyes flashed with anger. Jordan was Mr. Happy-Go-Lucky every time I saw him, so his mood surprised me.

"You must be Mr. Compton. I look forward to discussing the sponsorship with your esteemed company over the dinner that Pepper set up for us. I'm Stan White, the production manager here at the museum." He extended his hand but dropped it when he realized Jordan still had mine in his grasp and wasn't making any moves to let it go.

"Mr. White, I'm sorry to ruin your plans, but I made this meeting with Pepper. She's been my contact and I'd like to keep it that way." His words were cool and professional but his stare was hard.

"Mr. Compton, I assure you that my knowledge far exceeds that of Pepper's, so you'll be doing yourself a disservice by having her go over the specifics rather than myself. She's still green, fresh out of college." I gasped as Stan threw me under the proverbial bus. *Asshole.*

"Mr. White, I am feeling agitated and am now reconsidering

my decision to proceed with this. Now if you'll excuse me, I have other business to attend to." He squeezed my hand one last time and winked at me. My heart swelled at his defiance against Stan. Jordan began stalking off, but Stan called after him to stop.

"Wait! Sir, I do apologize. Please, take Pepper along with you. She could use the experience." Jordan nodded and waited for me.

I hurried to my desk and snapped my laptop shut, tossing it into my bag. Grabbing it and my purse, I headed for the door.

Before I made it all the way out of my office, Stan reached out and squeezed my upper arm, stopping me. "Don't mess this up Pepper."

From the corner of my eye, I could see Jordan glaring at him and taking a step forward. Stan dropped my arm and stalked back to his office. Jordan took hold of my hand again and I let him lead me to his car.

Chapter FOUR

Jordan

I NEARLY PUNCHED that guy in the teeth. He was being an arrogant prick, assuming I'd rather have dinner with him than the beautiful woman in the room. Someone needed to knock him down a few pegs. When he snatched hold of her arm, I nearly lost it. Thankfully he let her go when he did because I had been two seconds away from decking him.

"Are you okay?" I asked after we both got in the car and I put it in drive.

She sighed but nodded her head. "Yeah. I just hate that he treats me like I'm ignorant. Believe me, I am far from it." And I did believe her. She had the sexy librarian, teacher, professor look down to an art, and I had no doubt she could back it up.

"If it makes you feel any better, I was about to give him a bloody nose." She giggled, and the tinkling noise was adorable— so unexpected from her usual cool demeanor.

"Do you handle all your business deals with your fists?" she asked, raising an eyebrow at me.

"Only the ones worth fighting for." That shut her up.

We pulled up to the restaurant and I climbed out of the car, handing the valet my keys. I came around to her side, and she held on to my arm as I led her into the building.

The restaurant was nice but not over the top. We were seated at a corner table in a more private area. Pepper sat quietly, not meeting my eyes.

Finally, I couldn't stand it any longer. "That guy is a prick. If he ever touches you again, call me. I'll be up there in no time flat and I'll pummel him. Tough guys like me do macho stuff like that." She laughed when she realized my sarcastic tone.

"So, Jordan, tell me what it is exactly that you wanted to talk about over dinner. I'm still wondering why we couldn't have handled this over the phone." The tough Pepper we all knew and loved was back.

"Well, Pepper. Quite frankly, I just wanted an excuse for you to have dinner with me. All I want is to get to know you. My brother is dating your best friend. Wouldn't hurt for us to learn a little more about one another. Plus, you're fine as hell, and I needed a reason to stare at you for an hour."

Her eyes narrowed at me, which made me laugh. Those plump lips were pressed into a thin line. The eyes behind her glasses blazed with fury. She was so hot when she was mad.

"Don't patronize me. I know what I look like. People like you find something that's different than the norm, claim it, and then kick it to the side. Not interested, Playboy." Shit, she was something else.

I reached over and seized her hand. She tried pulling away but I held it firmly. If looks could kill, I'd have been dead in that moment. When I rubbed my thumb across the top of her hand, she shuddered and dropped her hateful look.

"Pepper, I don't know what you have me pegged for, but I'm not that guy. When I see something I want, I go for it and claim it. End of story. There is never any tossing it aside when I'm done. You're amazingly beautiful, and I think you're insane for not realizing it." I let go of her hand as the server came over.

We quickly told the server our drink orders and what we wanted for dinner. Pepper's face was expressive as something warred within her.

"In addition to my sponsorship, I would like to make a $200,000 dollar donation. Is there a way it could be made in memory of my father?" I asked seriously.

Her eyes flew to mine, and I knew she could see the heart-break on my face. My dad had left us in tatters when he decided that ending his life was the way to go. Our mother seemed to have handled it the best. Jackson, the worst. But then again, had I watched him do it, I'd be pretty fucked up too.

The tenderness in her eyes was not an expression I'd seen from her yet. This time, she was the one who took my hand.

"Jordan, of course. We'll even have a plaque made to hang in the main hall." She squeezed my hand and smiled beautifully at me. Good. I needed her happy, because this next part was probably going to piss her off.

"The other requirement to my donation is that you attend the gala as my date." The scowl returned and she jerked her hand away.

"No. I told you I had to work. There will be no time for social-izing. You saw what a jackass Stan is. He wouldn't allow it any-way."

I smiled at her. There was something behind that frosty exteri-or, and I planned on discovering it with or without her help.

"Too bad. You want the money, you get me."

She huffed but nodded, conceding.

The server arrived and poured wine into each of our glasses, leaving the bottle on our table.

"Jordan, I'll go as your date, but you need to know I won't be any fun. I don't do fun. Besides, I'll be working. You'd be better off finding someone else."

"I don't want anyone else. I want you." I stared her down with those words, letting her realize the double meaning.

She picked up her glass and quickly drained it. Not taking my eyes from hers, I refilled her glass.

Changing the subject, I asked her about her family. "So, Pepper, tell me about your family. Do you have any siblings? Are you from around here?"

She smiled and it actually reached her eyes. "Actually, I have wonderful parents who live less than fifteen minutes from my apartment. I have a brother, Will, but he lives in Paris with his fiancée. He's several years older than I am so we never really were close. I always feel like an only child until the holidays. My daddy is a partner at a law firm and my mother is heavily involved with her various social groups."

"So you're a New Yorker like me? I knew I liked you," I teased, winking at her. She giggled again and sipped her wine.

"Jordan, what were your plans before you were thrust into running your dad's company? I'm assuming that's right considering you mentioned your father passed on."

"You're right about that part. Actually, I always looked up to my dad. Jackson and I wanted to be just like him. Both of us went to college wanting to help him with his company. Jackson is the true architect at heart, and I'm more of a businessman. Even though I majored in architectural design, I took all of my electives in business."

"Did you go to Columbia?"

"No, I didn't," I said shyly.

She smiled at me. "CUNY is a good school too. No need to be embarrassed." Now I really was embarrassed because I certainly didn't go to The City University of New York.

"I didn't go there either. I went to school out of state," I muttered, trying to drop the subject. Pepper was used to being the smarter one of her peers. She already had me pegged as a dumb tough guy who'd inherited Daddy's company. Why change the stereotype now?

"Jordan, you're killing me. Tell me where you went."

"Princeton."

"Get the fuck out of here. No really, tell me where you went."

I just stared at her while she let it sink in. Her mouth hung open but she was smiling a really goofy smile, which made me laugh. So she had a thing for smart guys? Oh, I could be smart.

"Top five of my class." Now she was laughing.

"Jordan, you continually surprise me. I'll give you that."

When our dinner arrived, we chatted easily about college life. I discovered that she hadn't done the whole sorority scene—no surprise there—and that she'd met Andi her freshman year. She told me about the recent drama she'd been through trying to keep Andi on the right path after her breakup with Bray. I'd learned a little bit about that this afternoon when Jackson and Bray almost beat the shit out of each other over Andi. Pepper also said that Andi and their roommate Olive were her only friends. She seemed embarrassed about that. *More time for me,* I thought selfishly.

After a bottle and a half of wine between us, conversation was flowing effortlessly. Pepper was incredibly intelligent, and it was nice talking with a woman who actually understood everything I had to say. She seemed equally pleased.

When the server brought us our check, she tried unsuccessfully to take it from me.

"Jordan, let me pay. It's the least I can do since you stepped up to do the sponsorship." I smiled at her and shook my head.

"Pepper, this is a date. The man always pays on a real date."

She huffed at my macho attitude. After leaving a wad of cash on the table, I led her out of the restaurant and back to the valet area. We were quiet while we waited for them to retrieve the car.

Once back in the car, she spoke. "Thanks for dinner, Jordan. I actually had a nice time." She said it like she was surprised.

"Not all of your dates are that fun?" I joked, chuckling. She was silent and just shook her head, looking out the window. I reached over and grabbed her hand, squeezing it.

Finally, she decided to elaborate. "Would you believe I've never been on a date before?"

I nearly crashed the car as I looked over at her in shock.

"What? You're kidding, right? Pepper, you're a freaking knockout. Don't tell me you don't have the guys falling at your feet."

"No. There were a few suitors, but I always declined their offers. I would have declined yours too, but you tricked me into it."

I laughed, proud that I had done the impossible. "Pepper, let me take you on a real date. Tonight was mostly business. I want to have a night that's mostly pleasure."

She started to pull her hand from my grasp but I just gripped her tighter.

"I'll think about it, Jordan."

I'll take it, Pepper. I'll take it.

.

Chapter FIVE

Pepper

WHEN WE PULLED UP to my building and surprisingly found a parking spot, Jordan turned off the car. He seemed as reluctant as I was about ending the evening. His eyes lit up as he thought of something.

"Pepper, I just realized we never went over the documents. Do you think I could come up and take a look at those real quick?"

I knew it was just a ploy to spend more time with me. All he had done was come up with reasons to do just that. Nobody had ever pursued me this hard before. It was actually kind of nice, even if I would never admit it.

"Jordan, I think that's probably a good idea. I'll have to report back to Stan tomorrow, so I need to be able to prove to him that I can successfully do my job."

His eyes darkened at the mention of Stan's name, but he nodded.

We climbed out of the car and Jordan hurried around, grabbing my hand. For some reason, this felt comfortable. Maybe he was growing on me. Maybe it was the wine.

When we got upstairs, I was surprised that it was empty. I expected Olive to be there. Jordan made himself at home on the sofa while I poured us some more wine. Once I made it back to the living room, he'd already pulled my laptop out of my bag and was powering it on.

"Here, have some wine. Make yourself comfortable," I teased, smirking at him.

"Don't mind if I do," he agreed as he put his feet on the coffee table.

I sat down next to him on the sofa so I could better see what he was pulling up on the computer. Once the laptop loaded, I took him to the files that would show him what was part of the sponsorship package he would be privy to. We actually got through everything pretty quickly.

"Here, I want to show you something," he pointed to the screen.

I scooted in a little closer to see what it was he wanted to show me. He pulled up his Facebook account and located his pictures. The pictures of him and his brother were pretty funny. They were best friends—I could see it in their smiles. He came across another picture of a guy who looked familiar.

"Hey, wait. Go back! I think I know him," I exclaimed, but he quickly scrolled several pictures past and landed on one of his dad. They looked strikingly similar. His dad had hair the same color as his but it was streaked with grey. He was very handsome and fit for someone old enough to be Jordan's father.

"He was a nice-looking man," I told him, smiling.

"Yeah, he was a big hit with the ladies," he groaned, rolling his eyes, and continued flipping through photos.

I thought I saw another picture of that familiar guy, but he scrolled too fast past it. There was a niggling feeling in the back of my mind that said he was hiding something.

"You smell good," he stated, turning to look at me.

I almost spit out my wine and could feel my cheeks turning

red. The way he was watching me made my body ache for something.

For what? Jordan?

His hand came up to my cheek and he gently rubbed it with his thumb. I was frozen, snared in his gaze. He dropped his stare to my lips and then back up to my eyes. A silent question. I nodded almost imperceptibly.

He used his hand to guide me closer to him. My lips parted and my eyes fluttered closed. At first, the touch on my lips was soft, but then he pressed me to him. His tongue darted out and explored my own. His teeth pulled my bottom lip between them and nibbled. I moaned into his mouth. He groaned and stroked his hand down along my neck.

This was completely out of character for me. I hadn't kissed a guy since that horrific afternoon in high school. At least this kiss was enjoyable. Jordan was safe and protective. I could feel it.

His hand stayed securely on my neck, to which I was thankful. There was no way I was ready to proceed past what we were doing in that moment. His tongue danced with mine some more, and I sighed happily into his mouth.

When I heard the jingle of keys at the front door, I bolted away from him and off of the couch. I tried not to look guilty as Andi analyzed the situation when she walked in with Jackson and Olive.

"Hey, guys. Uh, Jordan, er, Mr. Compton and I are going over the sponsorship for the museum."

Jackson the Jackass laughed at us. When I stole a glance at Jordan, he was looking at me with a cocked eyebrow, which made me blush. Everyone was laughing at me, even innocent Olive. *Bastards.*

"Ugh. We were just working! You people suck." I threw Jordan a look that meant 'especially you, wiseass.'

"Our mother is having dinner at her house Saturday, Pepper. Would you care to join us? I'd ask Olive too but she has a modeling job," Jackson spoke, clearly attempting to help his brother. When I stole another look at Jordan, he just winked at me. *How can he sit there so calmly?* We had just been sucking face and he was acting all smug about it.

"I'm busy," I stated automatically.

"Liar!" Olive and Andi yelled, giggling. *Are they drunk?*

Everyone laughed when I glared at the girls for busting me out.

"Fine, but I'll find my own ride there and I'm not going as your date, Jordan." I shot him an evil look, but he ignored it.

"Come here. I want to show you something."

Figuring he wanted to show me more pictures, I sat down beside him and couldn't ignore the heat that poured between us as our knees touched. When he pointed to a picture on the screen, I leaned in to get a better look. It looked like a picture of... Agh!

He slung his big arm around me, pulling me to him, and planted an obnoxious, wet kiss on my cheek. I shrieked and tried to escape his grasp. His roar of laughter was infectious, and I tried to fight it but lost. Jackson reached over and snatched the laptop away before it became a casualty of our roughhousing.

When Jordan's tongue slipped into my ear, I cursed at him. "You motherfucker! Get your tongue out of my ear! Asshole!"

He laughed, removing his tongue. His breath in my now wet ear sent a chill down my body that I knew he'd felt. Everyone was laughing, including Jordan. All but me. I was a little turned on, but they didn't need to know that. That ache I'd felt earlier resurfaced.

"I'd love to show you more of what that tongue can do," he whispered into my ear. *Oh. My. God.*

After he released me, I punched him in the gut, rendering a howl of pain from his part. It was that or let him show me more of

what that tongue could do right here in front of everyone. Everyone else roared with laughter. *Glad we could provide the entertainment tonight.* The three of them finally went off to their separate rooms, leaving me and Jordan alone again on the couch.

Things got serious again when he looked at me. That annoying
ache pulsed through my lower abdomen. He did something to my
body just by looking at me. It was starting to get on my nerves.

"I've had a really nice time tonight, Pepper." He smiled, and I
glanced at those lips. Bad idea. I wanted to kiss them again.

Reading my mind, he used both of his hands, threaded gently
in my hair to draw me close to him. This time our kiss was more
fervent. Where the first one had been more of an exploration, this
one was full of desire. His hands moved to my hips and dragged
me onto his lap. My legs moved on their own accord to straddle
him. He groaned, and I could feel him harden underneath me. The
ache in my pelvic region screamed for a release.

His large hands gripped my ass and pressed me harder onto
him. Jordan was hot, funny, and intelligent. *Can the scared little
girl inside of me brave the possibility of something with him?* He
sucked on my lip again and I moaned. When he did that, I nearly
lost control.

He flipped me so that I was underneath him on the couch. Our
hot kisses continued. His hardness pressed into me through our
clothes. When his hand slipped under my shirt, I froze.

A tear slipped down my face and I suddenly felt nauseated. I
clamped my eyes shut, not wanting to see Cole's face above me.
Cole's cologne choked me and I gagged...

"Pepper, shit! Snap out of it!" Jordan barked, peering down at
me, his face full of concern. His thumb wiped the tear from my
cheek. "Are you going to tell me what just happened?" he asked,
sitting up so he could look at me.

I remained frozen on the couch, horrified at the memories that still hung in the air. When I shivered, he took my hands and sat me up as well. Drawing me close beside him, he hugged me. I could smell his delicious scent of soap and Jordan. No disgusting cologne here. I curled up in our silent embrace thinking about the safety I felt with Jordan. Sleep finally stole me away from him.

Chapter SIX

Jordan

LAST NIGHT HAD BEEN going great until Pepper had gone borderline catatonic on me. That woman was such a mystery to me. One minute, she was smarting off to me, as if she were the queen of the world and everyone else were just her minions. Then, she would surprise me and could be tender, even sweet, like when we talked about my dad. It was evident that the real Pepper was hiding behind the protective Pepper. As crazy as it was, I really liked them both.

When we kissed, I'd gotten to see the hot, sexual side of her. That side was my favorite thus far. Her body had melted to mine, and I couldn't wait to claim it. It was like she craved my touch. I sure as hell couldn't get enough of hers. But when I laid her down on the couch, things had gotten weird. The moment I'd put my hand in her shirt to touch her breast, she'd rolled her eyes back and turned into a ragdoll.

It had completely freaked me out. When she started gagging, I'd feared that she had been having a seizure. The tear that had escaped her eye had given me a brief glimpse into the woman that'd been protected by the icy, tough exterior. And fuck if I didn't want to protect her too. She'd not wanted to talk about whatever it was that had upset her, but I would get to the bottom of it. I needed to find out who hurt her.

The phone ringing pulled me from my thoughts of Pepper. "Jordan speaking."

"Jordan, it's Joel. Lou Jennings doesn't like your offer. He said you were lowballing him and it was insulting. He wants us to meet with him and his lawyer in person. I know his lawyer and he's a hardass. They won't leave until they get what they want. Just make the deal, Jordan."

My blood started to boil. I absolutely hated this fucker, Lou. How could my dad have even considered doing business with such a scumbag? Most people would have just handed over the money that was requested so that it would all go away, but I wasn't most people. I was a stubborn ass.

"Fine. We'll meet, but I'm not giving in to his full request. We've worked too hard to keep Dad's company running for some asshole to come in and wipe us out of all our capital. Set up the meeting. I'll meet with him and his lawyer."

After Joel hung up, I stormed around my office. Dad had really screwed us all over when he took the chickenshit way out. Clearly, between Nadia and these shady business deals, he had been in way over his head. *Thanks a lot, Dad.*

Later in the afternoon, I got a pleasant interruption.

"Jordan, hi," Pepper greeted, walking into my office. I grinned at her as she closed the door behind her. She looked especially pretty today but I couldn't figure out why.

"You look nice today, Pepper." She blushed but waved me away as she set some papers on my desk.

"Well, Stan wasn't happy about last night. He decided to take it out on me this morning by nitpicking everything I did. I just need you to sign a couple of these forms."

I scribbled my name on all of them and stood. She looked at

me like she was warring between kissing me and running away. Before she could choose the latter, I strode over to her and cupped her chin in my hand. Lifting her face to mine, I bent over and softly kissed her perfect lips.

Like always, she melted in my arms, which gave me the confidence to continue. Our kisses became more frantic and hurried. Her small hands slid into my suit jacket and rubbed over my shirt. All I could think about was how I wanted her touching my bare skin.

I broke the kiss and moved my lips down to her neck. When I sucked gently on it, she moaned and her nails dug into my back. Groaning at how turned on she was, I continued kissing and sucking her neck, looking for the places that drove her the wildest. Once I found a spot near her ear that made her pant like a dog and mewl like a kitten, I paid special attention to it.

Her hands slid up to the shoulders of my jacket and jerked it down. I shrugged out of it and yanked off my tie. My mouth found hers again, and I felt her hands go to the buttons on my shirt, quickly undoing each one. When she finished, I helped her pull it off of me. She pulled away to look at my bare, muscled chest. When her eyes met mine again, they were full of heat.

Her hands tentatively touched my chest. She was so innocent-looking and unsure. I put my hands around her and grabbed her ass, hauling her to me. Her hands instinctively snaked around to my back. When I lifted her up, she wrapped her legs around me. I walked us over to the wall and rested her against it. We continued kissing, and her body slid down, rubbing against my hard cock. She moaned at the touch, and I nearly came in my pants with need.

Before we continued, I needed to know what last night was about. I pulled away from her to look into her eyes.

"Pepper, what happened last night?"

Her innocent, sexy look transformed into a hard one.

"It was nothing, Jordan. Are you really choosing this moment to discuss it?"

"Pepper, you mean more to me than a casual fuck. I want to know what makes you tick. What excites you. What upsets you. What makes you *you*. Last night, you shut down emotionally. I need to know why."

She glared at me. Her chin quivered for the briefest of moments but stopped when she bit her lip. Her face was a lot more expressive than she probably thought it to be. Finally, she dropped her legs and pushed me away.

"I need to get back to work."

She stormed out of my office and left me half naked, with a hard-on, but most importantly, disappointed. Whatever it was she was holding back, I would make it my life's duty to figure out. She was worth it.

Chapter SEVEN

Pepper

"DADDY!" I exclaimed into the phone when I answered it.

"Princess, how are you?" his warm voice asked. Things had been so busy lately that I hadn't gotten over to visit him and Mom much.

"Great. I'm working on getting things ready for the gala. Stan has been unusually stressed and taking it out on me."

"I'm sorry, darling. I guess I'll have to come up there and kick his ass," he teased but continued. "When do you think you'll be able to visit your ol' dad again? I miss your sweet smile. Dealing with asshole clients all day means I really miss the sunshine in my life."

I smiled through the phone. Daddy was my hero. He always had been, and when he rescued me from Cole, it had solidified it forever.

"Well, I might be able to come to dinner tomorrow night. I can see if Olive could come too."

"Sounds good, honey. I'll tell your mother to set an extra place for her. Let me know if that changes."

After we hung up, the grin stayed plastered on my face. But when I saw Stan standing in my office doorway, it quickly slipped away. God, he was such an ass. Hadn't I dealt with enough ass-holes today? I'd already dealt with Jordan, who'd thought drilling me about my past was a much better idea than getting hot and heavy with me. *Whatever.*

"Can I help you?" I asked him in a clipped manner.

"Pepper, I'm sorry for being a jerk last night. You handled things well and even got a sizeable donation. I'm sorry I questioned your abilities. You've been nothing but a hard worker since you started here at the museum."

Wow. That was unexpected. "Uh, no problem. This museum is my life. Of course I'm going to do the best that I can. No worries."

He smiled, flashing his perfect teeth, and left. My life was just too weird lately. It seemed to be unpredictable, and I was having a problem dealing with that aspect.

I stroked Andi's hair as she snored softly in my lap. Olive had fallen asleep on the other side of the couch. These were my girls. Andi had been through hell and back, and Jackson still dicked her around. It really pissed me off. Bray could be the biggest ass on the planet, but even he was more likeable than Jackson. When Bray cheated on her and sent her into a spiraling depression that almost killed her, I nearly killed him. But at least he tried to be a nice guy—unlike Jackson the Jackass. I hoped that either Andi would get over Jackson or he would snap out of it and really love her like she deserved to be loved.

Olive's long legs were stretched out over the coffee table. The girl was angelic-looking. Her light chocolate skin was perfect and unmarred. When Andi brought her to the apartment that night a while ago, I'd wanted to say no. I'd been happy with having Andi all to myself. She had been my only friend and I hadn't needed some leggy goddess stealing her away from me. But when Olive looked at me with her doe-eyed, innocent expression that pleaded for human connection, something in my heart had acknowledged the kindred spirit. We'd brought her in under our wing, and it was the best decision we'd ever made.

Olive was such a fragile being. I'd always thought that Andi was the one who'd needed protecting and taking care of, but that was until I'd met Olive. Olive was almost childlike in her innocence. The problem was that her ex, Drake, had done something to steal that innocence away. I could see it in her eyes every time she looked at me. Sure, she hid it with smiles and jokes. But I knew the truth.

I thought that the reason the three of us had connected so well was because we all had been broken in some way. Andi had everything from her cold, distant family, the horrific breakup with Bray, and now the confusion that was Jackson to define the woman she had become. Olive had a prior abusive relationship—probably both physical and mental in nature—to define her as a woman. And me, I had to live with the fear of what Cole had almost done to me had Daddy not stopped it. It prevented me from being a normal person. Hell, I'd even embraced the shitty nickname he'd given me, preferring to use it over my own name. Every bit of what he'd managed to do to me in the span of such a short time defined me.

I just hoped we would all make it out on the other side. Happy, loved, and unscathed. *A girl can dream.*

My phone chimed, alerting me to a text. It was late so I was worried who might be messaging me at this hour. Pulling it from my pocket, I frowned once I realized it was from Jordan.

Jordan: Pepper, I'm sorry I upset you. I just want to know you. J

I wanted to say a lot of things back to him. *I overreacted. Or mind your own fucking business. Or find someone else to fix. Or I want you to know me too.* But instead, I just set my phone down and chose silence.

Chapter EIGHT

Jordan

WALKING INTO THE CONFERENCE ROOM at Jennings's Holdings, I nodded at Lou and his attorney before sitting beside Joel.

"Now that we're all here, we need to discuss finalizing these negotiations," Joel told everyone.

"I'm sorry about your father," Lou's attorney began, "but he began some deals with my client that must be honored. As you know, Mr. Jennings is a wealthy man. He's made his money by making good investments. One of his investments was in a venture your father started. Their other partner, who wishes to remain unnamed, also has a vested interest in what happens with this deal. Unfortunately, your father passed away before he could distribute the earnings properly."

I interrupted him because he was already pissing me off.

"Yes, it is really unfortunate that he passed away before Lou could get his money. So fucking unfortunate." My jaw clenched. These people were unreal.

Joel spoke up before I said something regrettable. "My client is upset because when we looked at the books, NAC Holdings wasn't anywhere to be found. This means the late Mr. Compton created this fictitious company in a fraudulent manner. You can understand my client's unwillingness to pay out on something that appears not to even exist. If you could allow us more time to re-search the matter, we would be happy to try to track down where this money went and funnel it on to where it goes."

Lou's attorney spoke again. "Joel, while this makes sense, my client is on a deadline with those funds. Mr. Jennings does not deal in illegal activities, so whatever you presume is illegal comes from your end, I assure you. All that matters here was that he was prom-ised a certain date that has come and passed, which has pushed back his other business deals. My client is losing money because of this foul-up. He is owed the 1.2 million and expects it immediately. And as promised, once the money is paid, the other two companies will drop their suits."

I gritted my teeth, furious. If we handed over that money, it would put our company in a precarious position, and I didn't feel comfortable with that.

Where did Dad put that money?

"I'll give you half now, and when I locate the rest, I'll wire that over as well. Give me two weeks to find it, Lou," I said, facing him. He'd been silent the entire time. "Lou, I'm good for it. I know Dad did some shady stuff, but I assure you I will pay out. Just don't kill the company in the process. Let me find it."

His features softened only slightly before he nodded in agree-ment. Lou's attorney just shook his head.

"This truly is against my client's original wishes, but we'll ac-cept your proposition. The time is ticking, Mr. Compton. Find it. I'll leave you with the wiring instructions."

When I got back to the office, I called Trent.

"Change your mind? The girl not worth it?" he asked, chuckling into the phone.

"No, man, she's totally worth it. I just got back from the meeting with Lou Jennings. This shit sucks. We've been over the books and I can't find what Dad supposedly did with it. They are demanding all of it but I talked them into half. I've already called the bank and wired the six hundred thousand to them."

"No shit? Well, that amount won't hurt the company too badly, but once you wire the rest, you'll be working with very little. If you all keep plowing ahead and business stays good, you might just stay afloat. What does Jackson say about it all?"

"Jackson is letting me handle it all. He's preoccupied with his new woman. We've hired a really good architect, so we should be doing well with gaining new clients so long as Jackson doesn't run him off for looking at his girl," I laughed. The whole situation with Lou stressed me out, but everything with Jackson was fucking funny.

"Sounds like Jackson. Better start looking for a new hire," he teased.

"No joke. I'll get right on interviewing some people. All right, man. Thanks for everything. I'll keep you posted if I find anything out."

"Sure thing. But, Jordan? Look into your dad's personal accounts. If someone was looking to hide company money, they might go that route. I'm sure Trish will cooperate."

"Good idea. Thanks again, man. Talk to you soon."

After hanging up with Trent, I dialed the florist.

"Upper East Side Flowers, this is Maude."

"Hi, Maude. I want to have some unique flowers sent to a Pepper Jones at the Metropolitan Museum of Art. Can you get those there today before five?"

Chapter NINE

Pepper

A WOMAN STOOD in my doorway with a dozen red-and-white-striped roses.

"Pepper Jones? These are for you." When I nodded, she set them on my desk and left. They were gorgeous and smelled like peppermint. I smiled because whoever sent them was very thoughtful.

Opening the card, my smile dropped.

Pepper,

I'm sorry if I offended you yesterday. Like I told you before, I just want to get to know you. I hope you like the peppermint roses. With a name like Pepper from a girl who chews peppermint gum like it's her lifeline, the roses seemed to fit. They're only half as beautiful as you. I look forward to seeing you at my mother's tomorrow.

Jordan

A tear slipped down my cheek. Damn him for making me cry. Every time I was with Jordan, he weakened the woman I'd tried so desperately to be. I was tough, bitchy Pepper. The girl who had embraced the hateful nickname from high school and wore it with pride. So why did it seem like he was siding with all of those terrible people who chanted, "Peppermint Pussy!" in the halls? He didn't even know the story, but I lumped him in the same category.

"I don't have time for this shit." I dumped the flowers into the trash and left work to go have dinner with my parents.

"How is your modeling going?" my mother asked Olive at dinner.

"Great. I have a huge gig for Express on Saturday. I am really nervous about it," she admitted, sipping her wine.

"Olive, you will do great. I think, if you will allow it, this could really make your career," I told her honestly. She grinned at me.

When we finished dinner, Daddy asked to speak to me privately in the study. The nervous look on his face had butterflies dancing in my belly.

"Princess, please sit down. I want to talk to you about something."

I took a seat in one of the chairs at his desk while he went around to the other side and sat down. His frown made me worry that something was wrong with Will or Mom.

"Sweetie, I'm afraid I've done something to possibly put you in danger."

I frowned because he looked really upset. "I don't understand, Daddy. You always take care of me."

"I know. I've always done my best to protect you. Even when that asshole Cole Stine tried to take advantage of you."

I shuddered at the memory and looked away from him. My hands trembled a bit so I clasped them together on my lap to get them to stop.

"Anyway, I know I told you there was nothing legally we

could do about what Cole tried to do to you. It was true. Nothing legal. But the more I thought about what he did, I was overcome with rage. I wanted to ruin his life. He nearly ruined yours. I can see that you still live with the effects of what he did. I mean, you go by Pepper for crying out loud. That didn't come from nowhere. My friend Dan, your history teacher in high school, overheard the awful things those kids said to you because of Cole."

I just watched as my daddy feared what he had to say next.

"So I pulled some strings. I represent the Chairman of the Board at Syracuse, where Cole's scholarship was, and he owed me some favors." He paused to look at me.

I swallowed, worried about where he was going with this.

"I spoke to him about the terrible thing he tried to do to you. He's got daughters of his own, so it didn't take much persuading to have him find a way to drop Cole's scholarship. I thought that would be sufficient, but the Chairman took further steps to contact all of his people in the education system. No college would give him a scholarship to play football. He was on his own and his parents couldn't afford to send him to the best of the schools. Cole was able to go to CUNY with the help of student loans, but football was out of the question."

My stomach churned at his confession. As much as I hated Cole and feared that he might try what he did to me with another girl but succeed, I still didn't like the idea of Daddy taking such measures for a vendetta.

"Daddy, I don't approve of what you did, but I understand you were looking out for me and other girls. So why does this put me in danger?"

His face blanched as he prepared himself for his next words. "Well, after checking up on him, I found out that he didn't last long at CUNY at all. He ended up dropping out and works through a staffing agency that places him at different places doing janitorial work. Last week, I received a letter that has to be from him. There isn't anything I can do because I don't have proof, but I think we need to take the threat seriously."

Threat? Mom's chicken pot pie wasn't sitting well in my stomach now. Daddy handed over a note to me.

Peppermint Pussy's Precious Daddy,

You ruined my life. Your daughter ruined my life. I will find her and ruin both of your lives.

You Know Who

I tossed the letter back at him. My hands, which I had been able to stop from shaking earlier, were now uncontrollably trembling. *What does he mean? Would he hurt me?*

"I won't let anything happen to you, princess. You're my little girl, and all I've ever wanted to do is protect you. As much as I didn't want to tell you about the note, I felt like you needed to know about it so you could be vigilant. He doesn't know where you are. Chances are, he'll look for your real name. Fortunately for us, you go by Pepper, which will stall him. I've hired a private investigator to look into him and dig out what he can find. If he so much as laid a finger on a girl, I will find out and we'll nail his ass to the wall. He won't hurt you, baby girl."

I nodded but couldn't help but worry. Cole starred in most of my nightmares. He always morphed from a nice-looking guy into a monster. It had all been just nightmares until now. Now, my nightmares were becoming my reality.

Chapter TEN

Jordan

TRENT AND I had been poring over all of the bank statements Mom had emailed to me earlier this morning. We were the only ones in the office, which was about right, considering it was Saturday.

"Everything looks normal," I declared, tossing a statement on the table. It was getting close to time to head over to Mom's. I really hoped Pepper would show up. She wasn't responding to my texts.

"Keep digging. He had to have put it somewhere. Was he a signer on any other accounts that maybe your mother might not know of?"

"Well, he was a signer on our trusts of course. He was the administrator."

"Do you have those statements?" he asked, excitement lacing his voice at the prospect of another avenue we could search.

"They're at the house. Why don't you go on home? I've got to be over at my mom's for dinner soon. Let's just meet back here tomorrow and I'll bring Jackson's and my trust statements. Hopefully we'll get to the bottom of this."

"See you tomorrow, man," Trent said as he stood.

I sure as hell hoped we would figure this out and soon.

"Mom? Where's my favorite lady?" I called from the living room. She burst from the kitchen and ran straight into my arms.

"I'm still upset with you, Jordie. You haven't visited in weeks. Jackson definitely moved into first place for favorite son."

I heard Jackson laughing in the kitchen at her proclamation. But I knew the way to her heart. As I held up the Godiva chocolates, she gasped.

"Who's your favorite son now?"

Mom snatched them from me, grinning from ear to ear, and everyone laughed. Someone knocked on the door, interrupting our silly exchange. When I opened the door to Pepper, I smiled broadly at her. She looked beautiful in her tighter-than-normal long-sleeved t-shirt and holey jeans. They hugged her curves, and I couldn't help but scan her body, appreciating each part of it. When my eyes made it back to hers, she glared at me.

At seeing Andi behind me, her face lit up, making my heart skip. I would have done just about anything to be the recipient of that look.

"Mom, this is Andi's roommate, Pepper. Pepper, this is my mom, Trish."

Pepper started to reach to shake her hand but Mom pulled her in for a hug. The look on Pepper's face was priceless. Clearly, she was not used to being hugged by strangers.

"It's so nice to meet you, Pepper. You are such a lovely girl. Perfect for my Jordie." She released an open-mouthed Pepper and hurried back to the kitchen. "Roast is ready!"

Pepper turned on her heels and pointed her finger in my face. The fiery glare she gave me had me wanting to kiss her fiercely. I couldn't help but drop my eyes to her lips when she spoke.

"This is not a date!" she hissed to me. I grinned at her because she was so damn cute when she was pissed. "I've got somewhere to be in an hour so let's get this over with. She then angrily huffed off into the kitchen.

Dinner was great because I could steal glances at Pepper while she ate and conversed with everyone. She even smiled a few times. That's all I wanted these days. I just wanted to see that woman smile. When she stood and excused herself from dinner, I followed her to the front door.

"Can I see you later?" I asked, looking down at her. She seemed affected by my proximity, so I leaned in a little closer. Her breathing quickened even though she still appeared pissed at me. Instead of answering my question, she asked one of her own.

"Who is the guy on your Facebook? I went on and looked at him because it has been driving me crazy. For some reason, I know that face, but I can't place from where."

I groaned because I didn't want to tell her. She was going to be livid. "His name is Trent. He's a buddy of mine from Princeton."

"What's his last name, Jordan? I need to know." She looked extremely angry at this point. Obviously my smart girl had pieced it together.

"Sutton," I sighed heavily.

"You motherfucker. He backed out of the sponsorship so you could take it!" she hissed under her breath, not wanting to cause a scene.

"Yes! It's because I wanted an excuse to see you. You wouldn't give me the time of day otherwise."

"You're damn right! You tricked me. That was so deceptive. Please, I would prefer if you would only talk to me about business-related things from this point on. I can't fucking believe you forced yourself into my life like this."

"Pepper, I did it because from the moment I laid eyes on you, you're all I can think about. You're beautiful, smart, and sassy as hell. I want you more than anything I've ever wanted before. There's nothing you can say or do to push me away. I'll continually pursue you until you're mine."

"Well, I just feel like a prostitute. A really expensive one. You paid seven hundred fucking thousand dollars just to date me. Do you know how insane that makes you? Step over, Julia Roberts. There's a new Pretty Woman."

"You are far from a prostitute and you're sure as hell no pretty woman. You're a fucking beautiful goddess!" I grasped her cheeks with each hand and pulled her in for a kiss. Her body lost some of its rigid fury, melding against mine, as her tongue darted out to meet my own. She tasted like wine from dinner. She was delicious.

Before the kiss could last any longer, she tensed up. Jerking away, she slapped me hard across the cheek and bolted out towards the front door. I grabbed at her hand but she yanked it away, and I was helpless as I watched her hurry away from me.

Chapter ELEVEN

Pepper

I COULDN'T CONCENTRATE during the movie with Daddy. He'd said that he missed me and wanted to spend more time with me, but I knew it was just so he could check up on me. The whole Cole situation had him freaked out.

Jordan was absolutely crazy. My blood boiled over with rage when I thought about what he had done. And even though I wanted to be pissed, I couldn't help but smile about it. For the girl who had never been popular and never dated, I'd sure done well for myself, catching the eye of the incredibly successful and sexy Jordan Compton.

If I were a normal person, I'd have done anything to date someone like him. He was tall, muscular, and handsome. That wasn't what made me attracted to him though. He was smart, witty, and funny, which were qualities the beautiful people didn't always possess. For someone who had the stress of a big company on his shoulders, he sure was a happy, easygoing guy. *And his smile.* God, his smile lit up the damn room.

Why am I being so difficult about everything?

It didn't matter anyway. Someone like him would lose interest in a girl like me. It was just wrong. I was pretty sure I was destined to be one of those lonely cat ladies. Too bad I hated cats.

Daddy dropped me off in front of the apartment and waited until I was safely in the doors before pulling away. Once I'd made it to our floor, I fumbled with my keys to unlock the door. I dropped them and stooped to pick them up. When I stood back up, a hand snaked around me and covered my mouth. *Shit! Cole!*

Screaming, I clawed at his hands as tears rushed down my face.

"Pepper! Chill, it's me, Jordan. I was playing with you, not trying to scare you."

My fear turned to indignation as I turned around and socked him as hard as I could in his face. The crack of his face against my fist resounded down the hallway.

"Fuck, Pepper!" he snapped, bringing his hand to his eye to inspect the damage.

I burst into tears because my hand fucking hurt. Nobody tells you that it hurts just as badly to be the one doing the punching. He dropped his hand and pulled me into an embrace. I dissolved unwillingly into it.

"Shhh, babe." He spoke softly and rubbed my back. The gentle move made me cry harder.

Why am I having a breakdown here in the hallway in front of Jordan?

"Let's get you inside, Pepper." He scooped up the keys from the floor and let us into the empty apartment. Andi was with Jackson, and Olive was working.

He led me to the sofa and I sat down. When I looked up, I realized he'd gone into the kitchen and was rummaging around for something. He came back grinning that annoying smile of his and set two wine glasses in front of me. After he poured some into each a glass—mine a little fuller—he sat down beside me.

"Pepper, I'm sorry I deceived you. When I did it, I wasn't really thinking about that. I just knew I wanted to see you and was willing to do whatever I could to make that happen."

I sighed and shakily took a sip of my wine. My tears had subsided, and now I just felt embarrassed for my meltdown.

"Babe, why won't you let me in?" His voice cracked a bit, making me look up at him. The emotion on his face made my heart flutter.

Jordan really was a good guy. I didn't know why I had to give him such a hard time. It was just ingrained in me at this point in my life. Even Daddy would like him.

"Because I don't know how. I don't know how to let anyone in. Andi and Olive only see what I want them to see and they're my best friends." My chin quivered, but this time I didn't stop it. He reached over and grabbed my hand.

"Pepper, I want to be that person you confide in. Please let me be that guy."

I smiled because he was one hundred percent genuine. "I'll do my best." That was my concession. It was small, but by the smile that lit up his face, you'd have thought I'd promised much more.

"Drink up, Pepper. We're going to loosen you up. Let's play a game. It will be fun. We can make assumptions about each other. If the assumption is correct, you say 'correct' and the turn goes to the other person. No harm, no foul. If the assumption is wrong, you have to say 'wrong' and the person doing the assuming will have to take a drink. Shit, we're going to need something better than wine."

I laughed at his silly game he'd made up on a whim. He jumped up and ran back into the kitchen. This time, he came back with a big bottle of tequila and two shot glasses.

"Jordan, this could get bad really fast."

He was doing a good job of distracting me from my prior meltdown. His playfulness was something that attracted me to him.

It wasn't the only thing though. His tight shirt stretched across his muscles and his biceps flexed every time he moved. Those were attractive too.

"That's the point, Pep." He winked at me, making my insides ache for him. "Okay, since I made up the game, I'll start."

He filled both of the shot glasses so we'd be ready.

"You're a daddy's girl."

I rolled my eyes. This was common knowledge. "You bet your ass I am," I confirmed. He smirked at me. "Okay, my turn. You're a momma's boy," I retorted back at him. He laughed because I was mocking him.

"You bet your ass I am," he teased. We both laughed. "You moonlight as a Victoria's Secret model," he pronounced, wagging his eyebrows. I rolled my eyes at him again. Someone just wanted to take a shot.

"Wrong. Take your shot," I ordered.

He knocked back the shot, chasing it with some wine.

"Your dentist makes you model your amazing smile in all of his commercials," I declared, teasing him and knowing it would garner me a shot, which I desperately wanted.

"Wrong. He doesn't make me. He pays me. Take your shot, woman," he winked at me.

I sucked down the shot and winced as it burned my throat.

"You loved the roses I sent yesterday even though you never thanked me for them," he said, smiling shyly.

I flinched. Then the answer was out of my mouth before I had a chance to filter it. "Wrong. I actually hated them. They reminded me of a time I wanted to forget. Take your shot," I spat out a little more harshly than I'd intended on.

He looked hurt by my words, and I instantly regretted them. I should have just told him thank you.

"I'm sorry. That was mean…" I trailed off.

He just shook his head at me and refilled our glasses. Tossing back his shot, he prepared for my next assumption.

"Um, you like basketball?" It was more of a question, but I figured I was safe with sports.

"Wrong. I like football," he answered softly.

I cringed when he said football. For reasons only known to me, I hated football. His eyes flicked to mine because he'd seen it. This man saw right through me, and it scared the hell out of me. I quickly drank down my shot.

"You like me but are afraid to admit it," he practically whispered. My eyes found his. When I didn't speak, my silence validated his statement. The corner of his mouth curved up into a half smile.

"The only reason you like me is because I'm different than all the bimbos you're used to dating," I snidely said to him.

"Wrong. That's one of the reasons. Not the only reason," he corrected. I smiled as I took the shot.

My body was really starting to warm up. Needing to cool off, I removed my long-sleeved t-shirt since I had a tank top underneath. Jordan's eyes fell to my tight shirt and hungrily looked over the swell of my breasts underneath.

"You took your shirt off to distract me from the game," he stated simply.

"Wrong! I took it off because I was hot," I told him honestly.

He drained his glass, never taking his eyes from me.

"You sleep around a lot," I uttered to him.

"Wrong. Not since college. I've only had a handful of girlfriends since then, and I don't do one-night stands," he affirmed, and my heart pounded wildly at his words.

I knocked back another shot. My skin burned, but not just from the alcohol. The way he watched me made me want to jump him.

"Someone hurt you. That's why you are so closed off from people," he expressed sadly. My eyes filled with tears, my silence once again validating his assumption. Fury crossed his features, and he snatched up my hand, kissing the back of it.

"Who fucking hurt you Pepper?"

"Cole. A guy named Cole in high school."

Jordan glared at me, waiting for more of an explanation. Squeezing my hand, he urged me to go on.

"I was a little nerdy in high school. Since I was shy, I didn't make friends. Like, at all. One day, the school's football hero asked me to tutor him. Of course I obliged. He came over that afternoon. Things were going great. When my mother left to run to the store, we were alone. He gave me my first kiss. Well, things got hot and heavy. Next thing I knew, he was on top of me on the couch. Things were progressing a little faster than I'd expected. He was being a little rough, and it pulled me out of the passionate moment. When I asked him to stop, he got pissed. It was then that he attempted to forcefully have sex with me. If it weren't for Daddy coming in from work and yanking him from me, he would have succeeded."

Jordan's jaw was furiously clenching and unclenching. He reached over and poured us each another shot. We drank them down because it was clear we both needed one to calm down.

"I've always been obsessed with peppermint gum. That day, he'd even taken my gum from me when we kissed. When I finally made it back to school, he'd spread all of these terrible rumors about me. Everyone thought I was some psycho trying to ruin his life. They called me 'Peppermint Pussy' because he told them if he actually had managed to have sex with me his dick would have frozen and fallen off. It was the stupidest thing ever, but all those half-witted people chose his side. The would-be rapist's side." My eyes filled with tears once again. I could feel his anger rolling off of him beside me.

"When I went to college, I vowed to be a stronger version of myself. One that was untouchable. When my new dorm mate Andi arrived and asked me my name, I told her it was Pepper. Short for 'Peppermint Pussy.'"

"What the fuck, Pe…whoever you are? I've been calling you Pepper, the nickname that asshole gave you. No wonder you hated the fucking roses! What is your real fucking name?" I could tell he was beyond pissed at me by the way he was scowling.

"It's Elizabeth. Andi knows my real name, but I won't let her call me that."

He rubbed his hands through his hair and looked back up at me. "What do I call you?" His voice was shaky, and the look on his face was sad.

"I'm Pepper now. At this point, if you called me Elizabeth, I probably wouldn't answer." My body was feeling really numb, and the unusually angry look on Jordan's face was turning me on. I reached up and touched his face. His features immediately softened. He leaned forward without hesitation and captured my lips with his.

It started out sweet, but we quickly couldn't seem to get enough of each other. Pulling away from him, still panting, I made a request.

"Make love to me, Jordan." I reached down and pulled off my tank top. Now he had a nice view of my taut stomach and my cleavage, which was spilling out of my lacy bra. He groaned as he drank in the sight. His hand gingerly stroked my skin, sending shivers down my spine.

"Not here," he growled.

I yelped when he scooped me up in his arms and strode towards the bedrooms. I pointed to mine and he flew in there, kicking the door shut behind him. He gently set me on the edge of the bed. Reaching behind me, he unclasped my bra and pulled it away. My heavy breasts bounced out. He guided me down on the bed and leaned over me. As he sucked a nipple into his mouth, I moaned at the touch.

He paid attention to my breasts for several minutes, kissing, sucking, and nibbling until I was nearly crazy from desire. My pelvic area ached like it always did when he touched me. His kisses slowly made their way down my stomach, and I gasped when his tongue dipped into my belly button. His laugh rumbled through my belly, making me throb for him.

Sitting up, he slowly unbuttoned the top button of my jeans and unzipped them. His gaze was hungry with a look that made me feel so desired. He slid my jeans down over my bottom and down my legs. Grabbing my shoes, he yanked each one off and slipped the jeans the rest of the way off. He knelt down in front of me on the floor and dragged me by my hips so that my ass was at the edge of the bed. Spreading my legs, he brought his face between my thighs and I rested them on his shoulders. His breath tickled my core through the lace of my panties. Nervous butterflies danced in my belly. I had no idea what to expect from this, but I one hundred percent wanted to find out.

He leaned forward and placed a small kiss on my clit through my panties. The simple touch sent a jolt of electricity through my body and I bucked against him. His hands found the tops of my panties and slid them off of my body. I was completely nude, giving myself to this man.

When his tongue licked between my folds, I bit down on my lip to stifle a scream. It was a slow, deliberate lick, and it almost made me insane. Deciding to skip the slow route, he began furiously licking and sucking my most tender area. I gasped and wriggled as he made my body shiver deliciously. His large hands gripped my hips, holding me in place.

The burn of something wonderful tore from my pelvic area up throughout my body, causing me to shudder wildly.

"Oh my God! Jordan! What the fuck was that?" My body continued to pulse and shake as I rode out the most wonderful feeling I'd ever experienced.

"That, love, was an orgasm."

Hmm. So Andi did know what she was talking about. The bitch really hadn't been lying when she said that they were the most amazing things in the world. I'd laughed when she bought me a vibrator one year for Christmas and tossed it in the back of the closet. I'd be digging that thing out later. That's for damn sure.

"Pepper, are you a virgin?" he asked softly as he stood up. His heated look was replaced with one of concern. I could feel my cheeks burning with embarrassment.

"That obvious, huh?"

"Yeah, kind of. Your first time is going to hurt, you know. Are you sure you're ready?" he asked. His gentleness about the whole thing made my heart soar.

"Yes, I trust you. You won't hurt me intentionally."

Chapter TWELVE

Jordan

IT WAS ALMOST too much to take in. The woman I had desired, pursued, and now captured was a virgin. And the only reason she was still a virgin probably was because that dick, Cole, had frightened her beyond repair. He'd scarred her mentally with what he'd tried to do and I hated him for it.

Looking down at her, I drank in her beauty. She tugged her hair out of her bun and dark hair spilled all around her. When she took off her glasses and set them beside her, I froze. She was perfect. An angel sent just for me. Her cheeks were still rosy and her chest still heaving from her first orgasm. She'd be having plenty of those now that I had something to do with it.

I yanked my shirt up over my head and her eyes darted to my chest. She bit down on her bottom lip, which made my dick grow impossibly harder. I unbuckled my belt and unfastened my jeans, letting them drop to the floor. Stepping out of them and my shoes, I slid down my boxers, revealing my very excited cock.

Her eyes widened as she took in the size of it. When her eyes met mine, I sensed a little fear. I crawled down onto the bed beside her.

"Don't worry, babe. It'll fit. We'll go slowly, I promise."

She looked up at me, and her fear was replaced with trust. My heart swelled. Leaning down, I pressed my lips to hers and we kissed at an unrushed pace. I slid my hand down to her clit and began working it again. Her moans into my mouth had my cock pressing into her leg. She came quicker this time and shuddered all over.

"I'm going to put my finger inside of you now. I want to make sure you're good and wet for me. Plus, I want your body to work up to being able to handle my size."

She nodded nervously, biting that damn lip again. Pepper was usually so sure and confident. Right now, her walls had dropped, giving me a glimpse of a completely different side of her.

I slid a finger inside of her, and she was indeed wet for me. She gasped at the sensation. Once I felt she was ready, I slipped in a second finger. Her moans were of pleasure, not pain. Curling my fingers to her front, I quickly located the nub of her g-spot. She jumped when my finger grazed it. Gently but quickly, I massaged it with the tip of my longer finger.

Her pants quickened as she neared her third orgasm. I knew the moment it crashed over her because her sex clenched around my fingers. While she rode out her aftershocks, I slipped in a third finger, feeling her stretch to fit them.

"Babe, I think you're ready for me. Are you on the pill?"

"Yeah, for my periods. Jordan, this is amazing. Thank you."

You have no idea, Pepper. "Listen, I'm clean. I make it a habit to get regularly checked. There hasn't been anyone since my last bill of clean health. If you're okay with it, I'd like to feel you without a condom. Do you trust me?"

She nodded and smiled at me. God, this woman was beautiful.

I spread her legs apart and positioned myself over her.

"Babe, this is going to hurt for the first few thrusts. If it gets to be too much, stop me. Otherwise, I will do it real fast to get it over with. You might bleed a little, but it will be okay." Her eyes widened a bit, but she nodded again.

I teased her entrance a little to get the tip of my dick lubed up from her own wetness. Once I was satisfied with that, I gently eased the tip in. I slid my thumb over her clit so that I could massage it while I entered her. I figured that if I could make her feel as good as possible, it wouldn't hurt as much.

When she started panting and grabbed her own breast, I slid my dick in slowly. She gasped as her body stretched to take my size. I could feel the barrier stopping me. Still working her clit furiously with my thumb, I used the other hand to grab on to her hip. With one hard thrust, I pushed all the way in. She yelped and a tear slipped out of her eye.

I leaned over, found her mouth, and kissed her gently.

"I'm going to start moving now, but I promise it will feel better soon." I sucked her lip into my mouth, and she moaned.

Slowly, I slid in and out of her. Even though it was painful for her, it felt fucking amazing to me. With every movement, her tightness gripped me from all angles. It was everything I could do not to come right then.

After slowly pumping into her, I could tell she was starting to enjoy it. Her hips were rising each time to meet my thrusts. I quickened my pace as I deeply kissed her. She lost interest in the kiss as her fourth orgasm tore through her body, causing her to convulse underneath me. When her tight pussy clenched around my already constricted dick, my come burst into her. We rode out the rest of our orgasms, and I finally stopped when the last of my come had poured into her.

She was watching me with a look of pure awe. I grinned down at her and pecked her lips.

"Are you okay?" I was worried she would hurt from not only having her cherry popped but having to take in my size.

"That was the most amazing experience in my life."

I chuckled at her words. "Just wait. It'll get better. Now that you're no longer a virgin, it won't hurt. You'll never want to leave this bed," I promised, wagging my eyebrows at her.

She grinned and threaded her fingers through my hair. "Sounds like a great idea, Jordan. When can we do it again?" This girl was amazing.

"Before you start making plans for the next love fest, let's take a bath. The hot water will feel good on any areas that are sore. And as much as I'd love to do it again right away, it may be too soon." The pout on her face made my dick twitch, so I hurried and pulled out of her before I changed my mind.

I tried to quickly drag her to the bathroom so she wouldn't notice the blood, but my girl was too smart for that.

"Oh my God! Did all of that come from me?" she shrieked, her cheeks burning red.

"It's normal. Come on," I urged, tugging her to the bathroom.

Chapter THIRTEEN

Pepper

AMAZING. FAN-FUCKING-TASTIC. I had so many questions for Andi the next time I saw her. Jordan was perfect. I wasn't sure why I'd fought the pull towards him all of this time, but I was a stupid bitch for doing it.

Once the hot water had filled the tub, Jordan turned it off and stepped in. He slowly dipped himself into the water and motioned for me to join him. When I eased my bottom into the hot water to sit down, I winced at the burn on my sex. Now I could see what he had been talking about. As much as I wanted what we had just done to happen again soon, I was afraid a little healing was in order first.

Once my bottom was fully submerged, I leaned my back against his chest. His arms wrapped around me and rested on my belly. We relaxed quietly in this position for some time. Finally he spoke, breaking the comfortable silence.

"Babe, you know now you'll never be able to get rid of me," he teased. His laughter rumbled in his chest through my back.

"Well, keep giving me earth-shattering orgasms and you'll be lucky if I let you leave the bedroom," I joked back. We both laughed. This moment was perfect.

The room grew quiet again. One of his hands slid up to my large breast and caressed it. The other one found my clit and lazily rubbed it under the water. My body started to pulsate with the now familiar feeling of the beginning of an orgasm. It seemed further out of reach this time—my clit was probably overworked—but when his pace picked up, my fifth orgasm for the night burned through me.

"God, Jordan, I'll never get enough of those. I feel bad because we can't do it again. And I know you need release because I can feel you pressed against my back. What do I do?"

"Absolutely nothing. I can wait until you're no longer sore. Come on. Let's get out. Trent's meeting me at the office tomorrow to go over some financial stuff, so I need to get up early."

Once dried off, we crawled, still naked, under the covers. He pulled my back against his chest, and we fell asleep curled into one another.

I woke up with a smile once I realized Jordan's heavy arm was draped over my chest. Last night had by far been the best night of my life. He had done everything in his power to not only make my first time memorable, but gentle as well. I'd felt taken care of. Looked after. Cherished. My body felt a little sore still, but my need to have him inside me overshadowed it. Turning my body towards him, I began kissing his chest. I slid a leg across him, resting my thigh on his cock. Already getting turned on, I could feel wetness between my legs as I softly ground myself against his thigh.

His chest was perfectly shaped with defined lines I wanted to touch. As I kissed him, I dragged my finger along the lines, tracing each one. I felt him harden against my thigh, which made me grin.

Clearly I'd woken him up. His hand made its way to my cheek, tilting my face up to his.

"Did you sleep well?" he asked, his voice gravelly. He looked incredibly sexy with his hair pointing in every direction. The hair on his face was stubbly and his eyes drooped lazily with sleep. I had to have him again.

"Yes, I slept amazingly well. I want you again."

His eyes blazed with heat at my words. When he made no motions to move, I quickly moved over and straddled him. He groaned when my wet pussy grazed against his very eager cock. His eyes devoured my naked body perched over him, and he eased his hands up to my hips.

Carefully, I slid him into me, causing us both to gasp at the sensation. His thumb found my clit. Rubbing it expertly, he drew me closer to my newly discovered happy place. I could feel the delicious burn start to spread throughout my body. Starting off slowly, I moved up and down on his cock. Even though it still stung a little from the night before, I was able to ignore it as my orgasm snaked its tentacles around me.

"Jordan!" I moaned as I threw my head back and rode my orgasm out. The hot gush pouring into me let me know he had come as well. We were perfectly in sync. I collapsed onto his chest and let him hold me.

We must have fallen back asleep because I awoke, startled by the phone ringing. Even though he wasn't hard anymore, he was still inside of me, and I smiled. The phone stopped ringing finally.

"Jordan, your phone was ringing. What time were you supposed to meet Trent?"

His eyes flew open in alarm. I unwillingly pushed off of him. He jumped from the bed and located his pants to retrieve his phone. I unabashedly gawked at his perfectly toned naked body. Redialing the number, he lay back down beside me. Unable to keep from touching him, I stroked my hand over his chest while he made his phone call.

"Trent! Are you at the office? Shit, man, I'm so sorry. Give me twenty minutes and I'll be there. Run downstairs to the café and grab us a couple of coffees. I'll see you soon."

He hung up the phone and looked over at me.

"If you keep looking at me like that, I'm never going to leave and Trent will be upset with me. You're giving me the 'fuck me now' face and I need to go."

I have a 'fuck me now' face? I must commit that one to memory and use it for the future.

"Sure, no problem, Jordan. I'll just use the vibrator Andi bought me. It's in the closet. I'm sure I can manage things on my own."

He growled and pinned me under him, causing me to giggle. His gaze was smoldering as he devoured my body with his eyes. Pushing my knees apart so that I was spread before him, he positioned himself at my entrance. My hips bounced up, begging for him to enter me.

"I think we have time for another lesson. This is what we call 'fucking,' and I think you're going to like it."

Without any more warning, he slammed into me, and I wailed in pleasure—and maybe a little bit of pain from the soreness. He pumped hard and fast, my tits bouncing with the rhythm. Another tantalizing orgasm sliced through me moments later, and he throbbed out his own hot release.

"Fucking is my new favorite subject," I breathily confirmed with a wink.

Chapter FOURTEEN

Jordan

WHEN I FINALLY got off the elevator, Trent was sitting on the floor outside of the offices, sipping on one of the coffees.

"Trent, I am so sorry, man. I finally won her over and we had too much fun this morning." I winked at him as I unlocked the doors. He stood up and handed me my coffee as we went inside.

"Don't ever apologize for getting laid. I'd do the same to you given the chance and wouldn't think twice about it. You two must be into some kinky shit because that's one hell of a shiner you got on your eye."

We chuckled and sat down at the table in my office. My sweet, feisty girl had given me a black eye last night when she punched me.

"Was she worth it? I'm thinking she was by the smile on your face. Plus, you smell like pussy. If you weren't into her, you would have taken the time to shower."

I laughed, nodding my head. "Oh my God, dude. She is the best I've ever had. And she's insatiable. I barely made it out of the apartment with my dick intact. If finding this money wasn't so important, I would still be there learning every inch of her body."

"Then let's do this. I'm not one to cock block," he grinned.

I pulled out the folder with Jackson's and my statements for the past year. Yesterday I'd printed them off but hadn't had a chance to glance at them yet. Trent took Jackson's stack and started reading through them while I took mine. About twenty minutes later, I came across something that looked weird.

"Trent! I think I found something. There's a rather large deposit to my trust about six months ago. And look, every month after, hundreds of thousands of dollars were being deposited. Trent, there's millions of dollars in here that I'm pretty sure don't belong to me."

He frowned and grabbed the stack from my hands. His eyes scanned over the deposits. "Let's look up the items in the deposit online. It might give us more information to go on."

I nodded to him and went over to my desk, powering up the computer. After an agonizingly long time, I finally logged on to my online banking and accessed the trust account. Trent stood over me, wanting answers just as much as I did. Once I opened up the items on the first deposit, my jaw dropped. *No fucking way.*

"Holy shit! This is fucked up, dude." Trent didn't know the half of it.

I scanned through the deposits and sure enough, Nadia Fucking Compton had signed each and every check. She was Dad's partner. Jackson was going to shit a brick when he found out.

"Thanks for your help, Trent. Now I need to figure out my next move. I'm considering hiring a fraud examiner."

"Jordan, I know you want to do the right thing, but that could potentially open up a huge can of worms. Are you prepared to lose the company if it comes to that?" he asked pointedly.

I rubbed my stubbly face with my palms, which in fact did smell of sex. "Yeah, I am. I've got less than two weeks to figure this out before I owe the rest of the money. Do you have any contacts that you trust?"

"I'll shoot you an email with the contact info. The best in the biz is AJ Cox. He's like a freaking hound dog. You can trust him."

I stood and gave him a hug, slapping him between the shoulders. "Thanks, buddy. I appreciate all you do. You're a good friend."

After Trent left, I called Jackson. He was going to be so pissed.

"Hey, Jordie, what's up?" his unusually chipper voice belted out. Shit, I felt like an ass for having to ruin his weekend.

"Trent and I went on a search for the money that Dad hid away. He was funneling money away in about a six-month time frame into my trust account. But, Jackson, you are not going to fucking believe this! Nadia signed every fucking check that went into the account!" I was shouting because it infuriated me that the bitch had jacked with everyone's lives and gotten away with it.

"Fucking bitch! What the fuck do we do about it? Are you going to give them the money since you found it? What's our next play?" He was frantic with his questions.

"Jackie, I'm going to hire a fraud examiner. We need to get to the bottom of this. If Nadia is involved in illegal activities, then she needs to pay. She has left a path of destruction in each of our lives, and I'm tired of her getting away with it."

"What happens if it's bigger than you think? What happens to the company?"

"Man, you need to be prepared for the worst. We might lose everything. I'm sorry, but it has to be done. I didn't work my ass off at Princeton to go down for illegal activities I didn't even commit. Are you with me?"

"Yes, of course."

"Okay, well, the next course of ac—" I was interrupted by Jackson shouting on the other side of the phone.

"What the fuck, Andi? I came in here to speak privately to

Jordan. You're being a fucking snoop!"

What the hell? Did he seriously just talk to her like that?

"Don't be a dick," I growled into the phone, hanging up on him. Jackson had better get his head out of his ass if he planned on keeping Andi. She was a catch, and his stupid ass could barely hold on to her.

Chapter FIFTEEN

Pepper

AFTER JORDAN LEFT, I stayed in bed, basking in our after-sex glow. I couldn't believe that I'd waited so long for such a fabulous thing, but I was glad I had. Jordan was worth the wait.

My phone chimed from the bedside table.

Jordan: Hey beautiful. I'm finishing up at the office and am going to swing by my apartment for a quick shower (since apparently I smell like sex according to Trent). I'll pick you up at 5. I want to take you on a real date. When I get there, come to the car. If I come up there, I can assure you we'll never leave. See you soon. ;)

I smiled at his text. This was what I'd missed out on for the past four plus years because of that asshole Cole. Normal people were attracted to each other, had sex, and went on dates. Normal people texted one another cute wink faces and their hearts beat wildly in their chests at the sight of those texts. Finally, Jordan was helping me be one of those normal people. Now, if my father could find a way to get Cole completely out of the picture, I would be able to move on and embrace my newfound freedom.

Me: I guess I'll put the vibrator down and grab a shower myself. Are you sure you don't want to come up?

His response was almost immediate, and I grinned at the power my words had over him.

Jordan: Dammit woman! I'm going to throw your vibrator out the window. At the very least, I'm stealing the batteries. I want to be the only one that gets the pleasure of touching you in your most sensitive place. We're going on a date so the answer is no to me coming up there. Don't worry though, I have plans for you later.

Me: Kidding! It's still buried under some old purses. I'll meet you downstairs at 5. XO

Jordan: I can assure you, your vibrator is no match for my tongue. XO

Now his words were getting me hot and bothered.

After showering, I decided on a pair of skinny jeans, a fitted sweater, and some flats. Normally I would just toss my hair in a bun, but today I wanted to be pretty for Jordan. I styled my naturally wavy hair to give it the beach wave look and left it down. I even applied a light coat of makeup, which I didn't wear often. Once I spritzed on some of the perfume my parents had given me for my birthday, I headed into the living room to wait for Jordan.

Olive was sitting, perched on the arm of the sofa like a cat, reading her book. The short shorts she was wearing revealed her extremely long milk-chocolate legs. Those legs would get her in trouble if she ever left the house. Men would line up just to have her wrap those beautiful things around them.

"What's up, Pepper?" she asked, looking at me over her book.

My lips involuntarily curved up into a grin. Damn Jordan for making me this way! Olive smiled back in wonder.

I heard Andi's door open before I could answer Olive, and she padded over to us.

"Not much," I told Olive, trying to suppress the cheesy look on my face.

"Wait a second," Andi declared, coming around to stand in front of me. Her hands went to her hips as she narrowed her eyes at me.

I bit my lip to stop any more damn grins that tried to give me away.

"No fucking way. I can't believe this!" Her voice was full of awe. "Pepper got laid!" she announced to Olive like I wasn't even there.

"What? I don't know what you're talking about!" I screeched as I felt my cheeks burn with embarrassment. Olive was watching me, her mouth wide open.

"Pepper, don't lie to me. You have that look that says, 'I just got fucked and I'm about to do it again.' Please tell me it was Jordan! Did he take your virginity? I knew you still had your v-card!"

"Andi, you are such a bitch. I don't have that face, but if you must know, yes, he took my v-card. Jordan took my virginity and it was fucking amazing!"

Like two schoolgirls, Olive and Andi shrieked at the same time. Andi made it to me first and enveloped me in a big hug. Olive wasn't far behind. I was grinning once again because it felt good to talk to someone about it.

"Oh my God, Pepper, this is the best news I've heard in a long time!" Andi squealed, hugging me tighter. I finally pushed her and Olive off of me.

"We need to know details. Tell me every last bit," Olive ordered.

"One thing led to another last night and he gave me my first orgasm with his tongue. And dammit, Andi, you never explained to me how fucking good those things were!"

"Pepper, you are so full of shit! Why do you think I bought you the vibrator? I knew you weren't getting any, so at least you could get a little pleasure somewhere!"

I laughed at the conversation we were having. Normal girls talked about their sexual experiences, and I was finally one of them. Even timid, damaged Olive wasn't a virgin.

"All I'm saying, Andi, is that you never told me about the earth-shattering intensity of them. You also didn't tell me that your body could just keep having them. And Jordan is hung like a horse. Not that I have anything to compare it to. Does it run in the family?" I asked, winking at her.

"Does what run in the family?" asked Jackson as he walked out of Andi's room. My face blazed crimson while my two bitchy best friends cackled.

"Nosy assholes," I replied snootily to him.

Rolling his eyes at me, he walked back into the room.

"God, Pepper, you don't have to be such a bitch." Andi stuck her tongue out at me and stormed after Jackson.

Whatever. My phone chimed with a text from Jordan. I hugged Olive goodbye and hurried downstairs.

Once outside, I scanned the street, searching for Jordan's car. "Hey, beautiful." Smiling, I turned around towards Jordan's voice.

He looked sexy as always, but this time I had a claim to it. His hair was styled in its usual messy way. He'd shaved the stubble from his face, giving him a sleek look. When he smiled, my lower belly ached. God, he was so good-looking.

"You clean up well," I teased. He cleaned up really well. And now that he'd stepped closer to me, I could smell him too. It took everything in me not to grab a handful of his shirt and inhale him like some kind of animal in heat. His smile was infectious, and I was having a hard time keeping my own in check around him.

"I missed you, babe." His hand touched my cheek, his thumb gently rubbing close to my nose. I closed my eyes, enjoying the simple gesture.

"I missed you too, Jordan." I felt his lips softly brush against mine before pressing harder into them. My mouth parted, wanting to taste him.

He understood my invitation, his tongue slipping in, tasting of toothpaste. Our kiss was deep but not hurried. My fingers reached up to his chest and slid down the contours of his muscles through his shirt. I felt his hands grip my hips and dig his fingers into me as he dragged me closer to him. Now that my breasts were pressed against him, my nipples hardened at the touch. A moan escaped my mouth before I could stop it, and Jordan jerked away.

"God, I'm about two seconds away from tossing you over my shoulder and hauling you back upstairs," he declared, breathing heavily. At least I knew I had the same effect on him that he had on me.

"Okay, let's go before I decide to encourage your inner caveman." Smiling saucily at him, I headed to his car. He opened the car door and helped me inside. Once he got in, his hand reached over and laced with mine, resting in my lap. The whole dating thing was so easy with him.

"Why does Jackson have a driver but you drive your own car?" I'd been going crazy wondering about this.

"Well, there's a back story behind it. When Mom was pregnant with Jackson and I was just a baby myself, she and my dad were having an argument while he was driving. A cab ran a red light right in front of my parents. Had he been paying proper attention, he could have stopped in time. Instead, they t-boned the cab. The driver was severely injured. My mom started bleeding, and they thought she was losing the baby. Turns out Jackson was okay but she'd had a partial placental abruption. Since she was close to term, they kept her hospitalized until his birth. Dad and I were unharmed. After the accident, Dad hired George. Growing up, neither of my parents ever drove. It wasn't until my dad's death that my mother started driving again. When Dad died, Jackson couldn't bear the idea of George being without a job. He'd been there our whole lives, driving us everywhere. So Jackson left him on the payroll and George started carting him around everywhere. Jackson's a shitty driver anyway, so it works."

"Wow. Jordan, I had no idea. I just thought he was an arrogant, entitled asshole," I joked.

"Oh, he's definitely still an arrogant, entitled asshole."

We both laughed as he pulled into a parking spot at a trendy little restaurant not far from my apartment.

The restaurant had an eclectic, bohemian feel to it. Every wall was littered with old records, unused instruments, pictures of local celebrities, and other oddities. It was charming in a hipster kind of way. The server—Glenda, according to her tag—was sporting dreadlocks and wearing a tie-dyed t-shirt and cut-off shorts.

"Hiya. The special of the day is Thai curry chicken with potatoes. Can I get you two something to drink?" she asked once we sat down.

"I'll take a Corona," Jordan told her.

"I'll have one too," I agreed.

The waitress nodded and sauntered off to get them.

"What kind of restaurant is this?" I asked Jordan. The name "Billie's" on the outside gave no clue as to what kind of food they served.

"I have no fucking idea but it's the best food around. Every time I come here, the special is different. I always just order what they're cooking up that day. We can ask for a menu if that doesn't sound good to you, but I promise that every single thing I've tasted here is awesome."

"No, that sounds wonderful."

After the server took our orders, we chatted about our day. I personally had a lazy day, but his was a lot more productive. He told me about how he and Trent had discovered some interesting information regarding his dad.

"I'm calling a fraud examiner tomorrow. Trent is worried it could open a whole can of worms, but I am not one to do shady business. My dad was an idiot to get involved in all of this. I want to find out the degree to how far this has gone and take measures to correct it. This company is mine and Jackson's now. Fraud isn't something we deal in."

"Jordan, that sucks. I'm sorry you're having to deal with it. What does the other guy think about you doing all of this?"

"Lou? He's given me two weeks to pay the other half of the money. I don't want to until I have the examiner look over everything. If he can't get it uncovered by then, I'll have to stall Lou. It won't be pretty."

I frowned, knowing that things could get ugly for him. I thought that maybe I could ask Daddy if he could help Jordan.

Glenda arrived with our food and we dug right in. It was pretty spicy, so we downed several more beers each. After dinner, we walked outside.

"What are we going to do now? Is our date over?" I asked, winking at him.

His mouth drew into a huge smile. "You are quite the minx. Don't worry, babe. I'll take good care of you later. There's a piano bar on the corner. I thought we could go have some cocktails and enjoy some music."

"Okay, fine. But you better make it up to me tonight. I can't stop thinking about your naked body. When you talk, all I hear is, 'Blah, blah, blah,' but what I'm thinking about is your tongue." Jordan burst into hysterical laughter, and I joined in.

"God, you are crazy. Come here," he responded, grabbing my hand and pulling me to him. He brought his hand to my chin and used his thumb to drag it down, causing my lips to part. His mouth descended upon mine and he sucked my bottom lip into his mouth between his teeth. When I whimpered with need, he unceremoniously wrenched himself away and started walking towards the bar. *Asshole.*

Chapter SIXTEEN

Jordan

SHE WAS DOING EVERYTHING in her power to make me want to fuck her on the damn sidewalk. When she came out of the apartment earlier, hips swaying in her tight jeans, I'd almost decided to can the whole date idea. She was worth more to me though. I wanted her to have a real date because she fucking deserved it.

After paying for our entry, I led her to a booth that was along the side of the bar but still had a good view of the stage. I waited for her to slide in first and sat down beside her so we could both see the piano. She ordered a Peppermint Kiss and I got a Vodka Red Bull. Once our drinks arrived, we snuggled together, waiting for the pianist to come on.

"This has been a nice date. I think I may get spoiled," she spoke, rubbing her hand along my thigh. The delicate pattern she was tracing along the inside had my dick trying to rip through the denim of my jeans.

"Babe, you really shouldn't start something you can't finish," I groaned as her hand now cradled my cock through my pants.

"I love that I have this control over your body," she purred into my ear.

The lights suddenly were eliminated except for the spotlight pointing to the stage. The pianist walked over and launched right into Sophisticated Lady. When I felt her hand undoing my pants, I jerked my head towards her.

"What are you doing?" I whispered.

She gave me the sexiest smile she could muster. "I'm satisfying my man. Nobody can see us. It's too dark."

I felt her slide the zipper down and my dick bulged through my boxer briefs, begging to be let out. When she wrestled my cock free, I nervously looked around. Everyone was looking at the stage. *Oh God!* Her tongue darted out and tentatively licked the tip. When I felt her mouth capture my cock, I groaned and threaded my fingers through her hair. Taking my noises and body language as encouragement, she bobbed her head up and down while she licked and sucked me.

Her teeth scraped me a few times, but it was hot as hell. A small hand slid underneath the shaft, gently stroking my balls, and I nearly came right then. I could tell she was testing how far she could take me because I felt my dick slide down the back of her throat momentarily before she pulled it back out.

"You have to stop or I won't be able to control it and you'll get a mouthful before you know it."

I swallowed my words as she swallowed my length. Finally giving in to my orgasm, I felt my seed pump into her mouth. She gulped it all down and slipped her mouth off of me. I released her hair, and she efficiently put me back in my pants, refastening them.

"Oh my God, babe. That was incredible." I was still panting and in shock. For someone new to the whole sex scene, she was catching on quickly.

"Was it now? I listened to enough of Andi's blowjob stories to figure out what you might like."

I pulled her close to me and marveled at how I had this smart, sexy, vixen of a woman who had no problems giving her man head in public. Finally, I'd gone and found the perfect woman.

We enjoyed the pianist and drank a few more rounds with our arms around each other. I hoped this would be a memorable first date for her. I wanted all of her firsts to be with me. She was a shiny diamond I'd found in a sea of rocks and I was going to treasure her.

"Let's get out of here, gorgeous. I want to spend some time with you. Alone." My eyes met hers and we shared the same heated stare.

Grabbing hold of her hand, I helped her out of the booth. The drive back to her apartment was short since we hadn't ventured out too far, and I was eager to get her upstairs.

After I parked just down the street from her place, we got out and walked hand in hand. The cool air whipped around us, but the heat that pulsed between us kept us both hot.

As we were about to arrive at her building, someone stepped out of the alley in front of us. The shadows covered his features, but he held something in his hand, pointed at us, that glimmered with the reflection of the moonlight. Tensing at the sudden appearance, I halted, drawing Pepper close to me.

"Hand over the purse, bitch," the deep voice growled at her. He took a step towards us out of the shadow, and it now became visible that he was holding a gun. *Shit.*

My hand squeezed Pepper's, urging her to do as he said. His baseball cap hid his features, but he radiated anger, which made my nerves rattle in fear for her. She was probably freaking out right now.

"I'll give you my cash, but you can't have my purse. My cards will mean nothing to you because I'll just cancel them."

What the fuck? Is she taunting this creep?

"I didn't ask for your cash. I said to hand me your fucking

purse!" He stalked the last few feet over to us and trained the gun to my forehead. The guy had a couple of inches on me and at least fifty pounds. Plus he had a gun.

"Sweetie, hand over the purse. Then the man can be on his way," I told her in a calm, coaxing voice. She wasn't thinking straight if she thought she could reason with a criminal.

She glared at him in a silent standoff, challenging him. I was scared of what he would do to either one of us if she didn't chill out.

"You've got three seconds before I blow his fucking brains all over the street. One. Two."

"Take it, motherfucker!" she spat as she tossed it to him. She was furious, and I felt her anger radiating around her.

He tucked it under his arm and walked away in the opposite direction, keeping his weapon aimed at us until he disappeared down an alleyway.

"Shit. Let's get inside," I huffed, dragging her into her building. Once inside, I grabbed both of her shoulders and made her look at me. "What the hell was that? You were taunting that lunatic! He could have killed us!" I was shaking her, trying to make her realize that she'd behaved stupidly. Criminals didn't negotiate.

"That asshole now has the keys to my apartment, my driver's license, business cards, and my phone. He knows my life now!"

Finally, I could see the ice crack. Her chin shook slightly and she bit down hard on her lip to stop it. She couldn't stop her eyes as they filled with tears. A tear spilled over and raced down her cheek.

"Shit, Jordan." The adrenaline was wearing off and the gravity of the situation started to sink in. I wrapped my arms around her and pulled her to me, hugging her tight.

"Babe, it's going to be okay. We'll change your locks. You'll be safe at work with all of the other employees. Let's call the police and make a report." I kissed the top of her head but made no moves to grab my phone and call the police.

"Jordan, why didn't he take your wallet? Doesn't that strike you as odd? What kind of criminal robs one person but not the other?" My mind raced at what she was saying.

Why the fuck didn't he take my wallet and phone?

"I'm calling the police right now. This is too fucking weird," I agreed, quickly taking my phone from my pocket.

Chapter SEVENTEEN

Pepper

FINALLY, AFTER THE POLICE had taken our statements, it was hours later and we were both exhausted from it all. After the police left, we spent another thirty minutes explaining everything to Andi, Jackson, and Olive. I was completely over it and ready for bed. Leaving Jordan in the living room with the others, I slipped away to my room. Throwing myself onto the bed, I succumbed to the tears that had been threatening me for hours. With my face buried on the comforter, I cried both tears of fear and anger.

A body joined me on the bed. The perfect smell let me know it was Jordan. He didn't speak. He just gently rubbed my back as I cried, which made me cry harder. I could have had him killed all because I had been stubborn about handing over my purse. My stomach roiled in disgust at my selfishness. Sensing my self-loathing, he leaned over and kissed my hair.

"You are a brave woman. I admire that about you." He was forgiving me for putting his life in danger. The man was damn near perfect.

That stupid asshole who'd stolen my purse had ruined our date. I wanted to make it up to Jordan. Finally, I rolled to my side so I could look at him.

"Jordan, I am so sorry. I feel sick about the whole thing," I whimpered.

His hand brushed along my cheek, and he grinned the smile that made my lower belly pulsate. "Babe, forget about it. I want you to stop worrying about it. It's over and we're both safe." He leaned over from beside me and kissed my forehead.

Suddenly, I didn't want simple cuddling. I wanted him buried deep inside of me. The connection we had while making love was one I craved at that moment.

My hand grazed his chest, sliding all the way down to the top of his jeans. He tensed underneath my gentle touch, anticipating my next move. I flicked my gaze to his and our eyes met, both of us pleading silently with the other. Before I could express to him what I wanted, he rolled over me, pinning me underneath him. His lips crashed down onto mine, and our kiss started out frantic and needy.

The hardness of his erection pressed into my pelvic bone through our clothes. Pulling my legs out from under him, I hooked them over his hips. He took the invitation to grind into me, and we both cried out in pleasure from the contact. My hips kept bouncing to meet him as he dry humped me.

"Jordan," I moaned as I broke our kiss, "I can't wait anymore. I need you right now."

"Good. I need you too," he agreed hoarsely, sliding back and onto his knees. He took off his shirt in one swift move, and my eyes dropped to his sculpted chest. I would never tire looking at his body. My sex throbbed at his perfect form.

Leaning over, he quickly started unfastening my jeans. While he tended to my pants, I pulled my sweater off and tossed it across the room. He'd already tugged my jeans down my legs as I un-hooked my bra and threw it away. I shivered when he stood and started undoing his own jeans. The little trail of hair above his waistline made me crazy with desire. My hand automatically slid to my breast and I rubbed my nipple as I enjoyed my private show of him undressing.

His eyes darkened as he watched me. He removed his boxer briefs next, freeing his cock. Taking it in his hand, he stroked it slowly as he gazed at me while I touched my breast. It was such a turn-on to see him touch himself that I wanted to soothe my own ache. My fingers from my free hand tentatively slid down to my panty line. I slipped my middle finger underneath and found the area that called for release. My clit surged with electricity as my finger flitted over it hesitantly at first.

"Fuck, woman. You are so beautiful. I could come just watching you touch yourself. But you don't want that babe, do you? Do you want me to get you off?" It was so hot when he talked to me like this.

Biting my lip to stifle a moan, I nodded. He grinned and eased his hands up my legs to my panties and pulled them off of me. My finger was still between my folds, but I was completely naked for him now. Drawing my hand away, he leaned forward and brought my finger into his mouth, sucking away my wetness.

"You taste so good. I want to take my time licking you until you come into my mouth."

I whimpered and spread my legs. His words. His voice. All he had to do was talk dirty to me and I probably could have orgasmed on command.

He roughly spread my legs apart, and I felt exposed, bare, and wanted his touch more than anything. Sensing my need, he knelt down and brought his lips just above my sex. His tongue flicked out and licked gently over my clit. My ass lifted from the bed, chasing his tongue as it withdrew back into his mouth. The combination of his rumbling laughter and hot breath on my sensitive area made me cry out for him.

I grasped on to his hair and guided him back down to where I wanted him. His laughter died as he licked me again, this time harder. Done with his teasing, he began an erratic pattern of licking and sucking. Whenever I would pull his hair hard, he would in turn suck my clit into his mouth, bringing me closer to orgasm each time. My body bucked against him with every suck. When a finger entered me as he sucked me hard, my orgasm hit me with such force that I nearly tore my calf muscles as my toes curled into the strangest directions.

Withdrawing his finger, he shifted away and looked at me with such a delicious combination of lust and admiration.

"I need you inside of me, Jordan. Don't make me wait any longer."

Not needing anymore begging, he hovered himself above me and pushed his cock up against my wet entrance. Wrapping my legs around his back near his ass, I used my heels to force him into me.

"Oh God. You feel so fucking good." He began rocking as he stared down at me, eyes ablaze with desire.

"Kiss me," I whispered.

For as quick as his thrusts were, his kiss was soft and gentle. I could taste my own unique flavor in his kiss. He sucked on my bottom lip, and I could feel another orgasm trickling through me, just out of reach.

Reaching around to his back, he grabbed my ankles and pulled them up over his shoulders. From this position, I could feel his cock dragging over my g-spot. Shuddering with delight, I allowed my orgasm to pour through my body like a rush of molten lava. My body clenched around him, and his own release fired into me.

He slipped himself out and crawled up next to me, draping his big muscular arm across my breasts. The events of the day quickly caught up to us, and within minutes, we were asleep.

Chapter EIGHTEEN

Jordan

MY ANGEL WOKE UP this morning in a mood. She was acting like the hardass she could sometimes be. She'd already taken care of canceling her cards and had also already made an appointment to change the locks to the apartment. Not having her phone seemed to piss her off the most. By the time I got out of the shower, she'd taken care of everything she'd needed to do as a result of the theft.

I was putting back on my clothes from the day before when she walked in with two coffees, handing me one.

"All of my credit cards have been canceled and thankfully there hasn't been any activity on any of them. I'm pretty sure all I had in my purse was eighteen dollars. It's all a fucking waste of my time." This morning she'd already been showered and dressed for work by the time my phone alarm had gone off. I could take a hint.

"Well, that is at least good news. Come on. I'll drop you off at work on the way to my apartment." I chugged what I could of the hot coffee before setting it down on the bedside table. She looked around for what I was sure was her purse before she sighed in defeat and left the bedroom.

Shaking my head, I followed her out of the room. I wasn't sure what had happened between our tender lovemaking the night before and the frigidness that rolled off of her this morning. My guess was that she was having trouble dealing with the events from the night before and unintentionally taking it out on me.

The ride to the museum was quiet. She wouldn't even look at me or hold my hand. It was torture for me because I wanted nothing more than to lace her fingers with mine and hold them in my lap. Her hands were neatly clasped together, resting on her thigh closest to the door. Again, I could take a hint.

As we came to a stop in front of the museum, she started to jump out of the car, but I seized her by her upper arm and pulled her to me. Her head angrily whipped towards me, but her gaze softened slightly as she looked at me.

"Email me later. We'll make plans for dinner or something," I told her and hauled her forward by her arm so I could kiss her.

At first, her lips were unmoving as she tried not to reciprocate. But when my tongue skated across her bottom lip, I heard her breath hitch. Her mouth parted slightly to let me in, allowing a small moan to escape. Not one to miss an opportunity, I kissed her hard and our tongues greedily touched one another's. I reached a hand around to the back of her neck while I simultaneously brought her closer and stroked her jaw with my thumb.

"Jordan," she sighed into my mouth as she pulled herself away. I let her draw away from me but didn't remove my hand.

"Email me," I commanded to her again. She nodded and I dropped my hand. As if to escape a magnetic pull to me, she practically leapt from the car and hurried into the building.

"Hi, Mr. Cox, I'm Jordan Compton from Compton Enterprises. Did Trent fill you in on the situation I'm in?"

I'd finally made my way into the office after a quick change of clothes at my apartment. Now it was time to get an appointment with the fraud examiner set up.

"Ah, yes. Mr. Sutton had only the most respectable things to say about you. I hear that you have your suspicions about some illegal activity that has gone on without your knowledge, which is having an effect on your company."

"That's exactly it. I'm not sure of all of the legal ramifications if indeed there was fraud going on, but I know playing dumb will only hurt us further. It is my responsibility as CEO to run this company in a legal, professional manner. That is why I seek your help, Mr. Cox. I need you to help me figure out how we can fix this without ruining everything." At this point, I was ready to uncover every last bit of any illegal activity and proceed accordingly.

"Mr. Compton, I assure you we will sort through this. If you were to turn a blind eye to all of this, it could haunt you later on down the road. At that point, you could be held legally responsible. Currently, I believe that, whatever we find, we can prove that it was without your knowledge and prior to your leadership. My schedule is free and I would be willing to take you on as a client. You can pay me a monthly retainer until the job is finished. My fee is $5,000 a month, and I can assure you that is more than a fair price. If that sounds acceptable, I can start tomorrow morning."

Actually, that was much cheaper than I'd expected, so it was decided without hesitation on my part.

"Thank you, Mr. Cox. That price is perfect. We'll see you tomorrow."

"Mr. Compton, I need you and your brother to keep this under wraps. Anyone besides your father who was involved will need to be exposed as well. If they know you're sniffing around, it would allow them to better cover their tracks. Just keep my involvement discreet. Call a meeting with the other party that is requesting the debt resolution. I'll have a list of questions for you to try and work into conversation. This will help as I attempt to uncover the truth. Again, Mr. Compton, utmost discretion."

"Thank you, Mr. Cox. I will advise Jackson as well. See you tomorrow."

After hanging up the phone, I checked my emails and smiled at seeing that there was one from Pepper.

Jordan,

I miss Andi. Since I still don't have anything to wear for the gala on Thursday, we've decided to have dinner and go shopping. I need a new purse anyway. I'd say call me later but I don't have a phone. Want to meet for lunch tomorrow?

Pepper

I could tell when I was being avoided. Pepper was withdrawing from me and it fucking sucked. Clearly she needed some space, and even though I was unhappy about it, I would give it to her.

Pepper,

Lunch is fine. I equally miss my brother.

Jordan

Rising from my chair, I walked over to Jackson's office. Bray was at Andi's desk, discussing one of his clients with her. From the sound of it, he was trying to talk her into going with him to meet a new client and she was looking for any excuse not to. Walking into Jackson's office, I closed the door behind me.

"Jackie!" I greeted, striding over to his desk and sinking into one of his guest chairs.

"What's up, Jordie? Hear anything from Mr. Cox?" he asked.

"Yeah. Actually he's coming in tomorrow. He wants us to keep a lid on his involvement in an effort to uncover any leads to other guilty parties that were a part of it. We already know Nadia's been signing the checks going into my trust. If we want to discover her participation, then we need to keep it quiet. I'm going call Lou shortly and see about meeting with him tomorrow. If Mr. Cox is going to properly help us, I need to stall for more time. I'm not willing to spend another fucking dime 'til we get to the bottom of this. I just have to tread lightly so I don't piss Lou off."

"Okay. I can keep quiet. Andi's going shopping with Pepper tonight. You want to hit the gym after work?"

"Let's do it."

Chapter NINETEEN

Pepper

"TRY THIS ONE," Andi instructed, dropping a red heap of silky material over the dressing room door. She'd made me try on at least fifteen different dresses and I was getting bored. This gala was way out of my comfort zone, but it was a necessary part of my job.

Slipping it up over my hips and then shoulders, I admired how I looked. The material hugged every curve, making me look more voluptuous than I had ever seen myself to be. The neckline was low but not slutty. None of the other dresses had caught my eye. In fact, I really didn't care what I wore. But now that I saw myself in this red beauty, I knew it was the one.

Spinning to see the back, I reminded myself I was going to be there for work, not socializing, even if Jordan did call it a date. He was going to be rudely awakened when I wasn't by his side the whole time.

There was something certifiably wrong with me when it came to Jordan. This great, hot-as-hell guy was completely into me and I just felt the need to push him away.

Mostly, I wanted to slow things down. After the mugging, I started piecing together some ideas that maybe Cole was the perpetrator. It was strangely coincidental that the day after Daddy told me about Cole's vendetta I was robbed by a really large guy who could have fit his profile. It would have seemed like a fluke had the guy taken Jordan's wallet too. Since he had only been interested in my purse, which housed identification that would prove who I was, the signs pointed to him.

"How does it look?" Andi asked from the other side, interrupting my thoughts.

"I need you to zip me up, but I actually think it looks nice." Unlocking the door, I pushed it open for her to come inside. When she saw me, she gasped as her eyes perused my body.

"Nice? Cut the crap, Pepper. You look gorgeous! Jordan is going to shit himself when he sees you in that dress!"

I frowned at the mention of his name, but she was too busy checking me out to notice. Hurrying over to me, she zipped up the dress. We looked into the mirror together, and I actually felt sexy for once in my life.

"Andi, let me use your phone. I'm going to ask my mom if I can borrow some of her jewelry. She is forever going to fancy events, and I bet she'll have something to go with this."

She handed it over to me, and I smiled at my reflection as it rang. The dress went all the way to the floor, so I would need to wear high heels. I bet Andi had something I could use.

"Andi darling, how are you?" my mother breezily asked into the phone.

"Mom, it's me, Pepper. I'm calling from Andi's phone. Mine is being replaced."

"Hi, sweetie. Everything okay?" she asked, concern lacing her voice.

"Yeah, everything's fine. I was wondering if I could borrow some jewelry for the gala Thursday night. Andi and I just found the perfect dress, but it just needs a little something extra to complete the look."

"Why of course, darling. Will you have a date?" she questioned in a hopeful tone that made me feel guilty for not ever trying to date after the Cole incident.

"Actually, I do have a date. We're sort of casually seeing each other, but he's a good guy. You and Daddy would like him. I think everyone likes him." I hadn't meant to tell her about Jordan, but I wanted to make her proud.

"Oh my God, Elizabeth! This is exciting news. You must bring him for dinner tomorrow evening. We'll rifle through my jewelry then. Text me a picture so I can pull some pieces that might work." She was talking excitedly, and I wasn't about to correct her for calling me Elizabeth. If anyone could get away with calling me that, it would be Mom.

"I'll ask him. I can't promise that he won't be busy, but we'll see. See you tomorrow, Mom. Love you."

"Love you too, hon."

After I hung up, I handed the phone back to Andi so she could take a picture to send to Mom.

"Let's get this bought and run by the apartment to drop it off. The margaritas at dinner were great, but I want to have some more drinks with my best friend. We need to catch up. I need to hear more about you and Jordan," she said eagerly.

I rolled my eyes because I didn't know how to explain how I felt about things right now. "Fine, whatever. Do you have shoes that will go with this?" I was trying to change the subject about Jordan.

"Pepper, does the desert have sand?" she laughed as she unzipped my dress. When my dress fell to the floor, her eyes skittered over me.

"You're worse than a man, Andi," I declared, pulling my jeans back on.

"What? A woman can appreciate another woman's beauty. Pepper, you have a rocking body that nobody ever gets to see. I bet Jordan can't get enough of you. You definitely were born to be a Victoria's Secret model. Ooh, maybe Olive can get you the hookup into the industry," she teased, wagging her eyebrows at me.

"I'd die a thousand brutal deaths before I even considered the possibility of ever doing that."

Giggling, she slapped me on the ass and left the dressing room. God, she was such weirdo sometimes.

Chapter TWENTY

Jordan

AFTER OUR WORKOUT and dinner, I drove us over to Dempsey's. We both wanted to catch up with our friend Ian, and I needed a drink.

"Jackson, Jordan!" Ian called from the bar as we walked inside.

"What's up, man?" I patted him on the back when he walked up to me.

"Another slow Monday. I'm going to have to figure out a way to bring more business in otherwise I'll have to close on Monday nights."

"I'm sure you'll figure something out, man."

While Ian took off to get us some drinks, Jackson and I sat down at a corner booth.

"So what's up with you and Pepper?" Jackson finally asked. I'd hoped he had been too preoccupied with gushing about Andi to bring light to my relationship with Pepper.

"Honestly, I don't know what the fuck's up with her. Ever since she woke up this morning, she's been avoiding me. I think she's still in shock from yesterday's mugging. Jackie, she's amazing in bed, but with her, it's more than that. She's a mystery to me, and I want to discover everything about her. Every time I take a step forward with her, I feel like she takes two steps back. All I do is fucking chase her," I told him in frustration.

"From what Andi tells me, she's very inexperienced. Maybe you just need to be patient with her. Is she even worth the chase? She's been nothing but a bitch to me," Jackson clipped out in a tone that was meant to piss me off.

"Don't fuck with me, dude. Of course she's worth the chase. She's all I can think about. I just wish I could convince her to trust me. Pepper likes to put up walls, and it pisses me off that she puts them up for me too. I thought after we finally made love, she would have dropped them. At least with me."

Jackson started laughing, and I glared back at him.

"What the hell, man? What's so funny? I'm fucking pouring my heart out here and you're laughing your ass off," I huffed.

"Well, for one, you sound like a sissy. 'We made love, blah, blah, blah.' Second, she's walking over here with Andi and she has her signature bitch face on."

I whipped around in the booth as the girls walked up. Andi flew into the booth on Jackson's side, practically mauling him. Those two needed to get a room.

Stepping up from the booth, I pulled Pepper into a hug. She remained tense and didn't hug me back.

What the fuck is her deal?

"Please, sit down. How was the dress shopping? I see you got a new purse. Looks nice."

She gave me a tight smile and reluctantly scooted into the booth. I glanced over at Ian, who nodded, letting me know that he'd bring them a drink as well.

Finally pulling her lips from Jackson, Andi spoke to me.

"Jordan, you are going to die when you see Pepper in that dress. I almost went lesbian on her because she looked so hot!"

Jackson grabbed Andi's thigh, making her squeal. He was jealous of a fucking girl. My brother had issues.

"I'm sure she will be breathtakingly beautiful," I assured Andi.

Pepper tensed beside me, and it took everything in me not to snatch her hand into mine.

Ian set our drinks down, but a crowd of about ten people walked in at that moment so he didn't get to hang around.

"Where's Olive?" Jackson asked the girls.

Pepper remained silent and withdrawn so Andi answered.

"She didn't feel like going out. Poor girl doesn't handle social settings well. For my birthday on Wednesday, we figured we'll do something at the apartment so Olive can be a part of it. Of course, both of you guys are invited. I'm even going to invite Bray." Jackson grumbled something and rolled his eyes. She continued. "I'm going to invite Bray because Dr. Sweeney thinks he and Jackson could benefit from attempting to be friends or, at the very least, friendly."

I nodded my head, agreeing with her. We were stuck with Bray for a year by contract. He already was proving himself with the few big clients he'd landed recently. It would only help our company to have a strong architect like Bray. Jackson needed to get over himself. I certainly couldn't handle them getting into pissing matches every time I turned around. The air had been pretty thick with tension today as those two had avoided each other as much as possible for guys who had side-by-side offices. It was incredibly awkward for everyone, especially Andi.

"I didn't realize your birthday was Wednesday, Andi. Of course I'll be there," I promised, garnering a huge grin from her.

Pepper sighed loudly, and I snapped my head to her. Out of the corner of my eye, I saw Jackson practically sucking off Andi's face.

"Okay, what's going on? Last night we were fine and this morning we're not. You've successfully managed to avoid me all day, and I'm sitting here dumbfounded as to why. Did I do something to upset you?" My voice was a little on the pathetic side.

For the briefest of seconds, I saw it. Her telltale chin quiver. I thought she was going to bite her lip to stop it, but instead, she pressed them into a tight line.

"Jordan, it's nothing. Maybe we just need to slow things down." Her face was telling me that she was serious, but her eyes alluded to the fact that she didn't quite believe what she was saying.

Interrupting us from our stare down, Andi spoke to us.

"Um, Jackson just texted George to come get us. We're going to his place. He missed me. Jordan, can you take Pepper home?" she questioned, face flushed.

Jackson just smiled at us with his shit-eating grin he'd perfected.

Not caring what kind of answer Pepper was about to give, I answered Andi quickly. "Of course I don't mind. I'll get her back safely," I promised.

They both waved and rushed outside, probably eager to attack each other. I couldn't help but feel a pang of jealousy of their easy, lighthearted relationship. Everything with Pepper was difficult.

"Want another drink?" I asked her once they left.

She shook her head, sipping the one in her hand. This silent treatment and cool aloofness was getting on my nerves.

Her hair was piled up on her head, so when I dipped my head down to her neck, I had easy access to her skin. Gently, I pressed my lips right along the side. A shiver, one she couldn't control, rolled through her. She started to say something and pull away, but when my tongue gently dragged over the area, she relaxed, leaning closer to me.

Taking it as permission, I softly sucked her into my mouth. Her whimper encouraged me even more. I slid my hand to her leg and skimmed it along her upper thigh.

"Jordan," she whispered.

My fingers rubbed along the seam of her jeans but stopped before touching her where she really wanted me. When I moved them back toward her knee, she mewled at the loss. Reaching her knee, I brought them back along the inside of her thigh, again stopping before I got to where she burned for me. Her breaths were coming hard and heavy. I repeated the motion with my fingers several more times while I suckled her neck, and I thought she was going to come without me ever even having to touch her there at all.

"Pepper, do you want to come home with me?"

She didn't respond at first, and I felt like she was warring with herself on the matter. Finally, the side of her that wanted me won because she nodded almost imperceptibly. I rewarded her answer my dragging my thumb across her clit through her jeans. She moaned but quickly bit her lip to stifle it.

"Let's get out of here, babe," I told her, chuckling as I tugged her out of the booth with me, not giving her time to recover or change her mind.

Chapter TWENTY-ONE

Pepper

I WAS A WEAK person. Jordan was like kryptonite to me. Whenever he wasn't around, I could be the badass I was used to being. But the moment he touched me, I was useless. No matter how resolved I was to slowing things down, it all went away the moment our skin connected. Our touch was always laced with burning electricity, and I was powerless against it.

The newly awakened sexual part of me wanted to wrap her legs around him and latch on forever. My practical self was screaming at me to chill out, because without my "Pepper the Bitch" façade, I wasn't quite sure who I was supposed to be. Jordan made a practice of putting cracks into my icy exterior, and it unnerved me. If I dropped that part of me, I would be left with the real me. The real me who was shy, nervous around people, and way too trusting. I couldn't stand that girl, which fueled the need to keep him at arm's length.

When we drove past my apartment, I looked at him questioningly. He brought our joined hands together and kissed the back of mine.

"I'm taking you to my place."

I was kind of curious about his place anyway. He'd been to

my apartment several times, but I'd yet to see his. In reality, I knew nothing about him besides what he did for a living and that he was a fantastic lover.

"Okay, but what about work tomorrow?" I questioned.

"We'll get up early so I can run you home to get ready for work. I want you in my bed."

His words made me shiver again. Damn him and his control over my body. I couldn't argue though with the fact that I wanted to be in his bed too. My plan was failing miserably.

He turned into a parking garage and found what I assumed was an assigned spot. We got out, and he held his hand out to me when he made his way to my side of the car. Like the sucker I was, I reached out and clasped mine to his.

The elevator had to be accessed by a code, and we rode to the eight floor. When we stepped out, we went down a hallway to the end, and he unlocked his door, motioning me inside.

He found a light in the entryway and switched it on, illuminating the way into the living room. His apartment was messy, which kind of shocked me. It wasn't gross. He just had a lot of stuff. The apartment was definitely lived in.

Books littered the room. He had stacks of them on tables, shelves, and even the coffee table. Jordan clearly loved to read. My heart swelled a little when I was reminded that he was more than just a pretty face. I walked over and picked up the first book within reach.

"The Count of Monte Cristo by Alexandre Dumas?" I inquired, holding it up.

"The book is better than the movie, I assure you, babe," he teased me.

My eyes skittered to all of the photos he had in mismatched frames all over the place. There was a large one on the mantle that caught my eye. Jordan and Jackson were younger, probably late teens, and their Dad was between them with an arm draped over each of them. They were so happy, and it made my heart hurt for him.

"I'm going to get us some wine," he told me, walking into the kitchen.

I continued checking out his apartment. He had a massive desk adorned with a really expensive Mac with a huge screen over in the corner. His apartment might have been on the unusually homey side, but his desk was one that a successful man would be expected to use. Blueprints were stacked all over the desk in an untidy way. The framed picture of him and his mom beside his monitor made me smile. Jordan adored his family, which was evident.

"Here, babe," he said, handing me a glass. His made-to-look-messy hair and panty-dropping grin had my insides trembling.

Looking away, I drained half my glass. Jordan was so good-looking it hurt. This was exactly why I couldn't figure out who I was supposed to be anymore. Around him, I turned into a giggly, boy-crazy girl. It was rather annoying.

"Pepper, come sit down with me. Let's talk about what's going on with you." He guided me to the sofa and we sat down beside each other. His arm slipped behind me, gripping my hip, and held me close to him.

"Jordan, it's nothing," I replied, hoping to deter his inquiries.

"Babe, don't lie to me. Just tell me what's going on inside that head of yours. I know you want me by the way you respond to my touch," he declared as he proved his point by rubbing my hip through my clothes. When a finger slipped under my sweater and gently stroked the skin above my jeans, I started to breathe heavily.

He continued his observations. "But the moment I step away from you, I feel you withdrawing from me. I don't understand it, Pepper." His finger continued to trace a line back and forth along the top of my pants.

"Jordan, I'll tell you the truth. I don't like the person I am with you. I'm weak and vulnerable. Today I came to the realization that I may have been mugged by Cole, the ass that almost raped me in high school. It made me think that I need to keep my guard up because of his threats to hurt me. When I'm around you, I get fucking giddy, and last night just proved that it opens me up for harm from him."

"Dammit, Pepper! Why didn't you tell me that you thought it was him? And what threats are you talking about? We should call the police about this. I'm sure they could do something about it. You can't let him dictate your life."

I frowned. "It isn't that easy. My daddy kind of went out of his way to ruin Cole's life and now he's got a vendetta. Saturday night, Daddy told me Cole had sent a threatening letter. That's why I freaked when you grabbed me that night."

He jumped from the couch and ran his fingers through his thick hair. Immediately, he started pacing the room.

"Pepper, we have to do something. That prick had a gun if that was him. Fuck! That's why he took your purse and not my wallet. Tomorrow, you have to call the police."

I furiously sprang to my feet.

"And tell them what, Jordan? We have no proof. He didn't succeed in fucking me. He didn't sign the letter. He didn't show his face last night. I have nothing."

He stormed over to me and took my face into his hands, scowling at me.

"I don't fucking know, Pepper, but I won't let you push me away. You're mine and I'm not letting you drive me away!"

"Yours? I don't belong to anybody!" I screeched at him, jerking away.

Lightning fast, his arms enveloped me and pulled me in for a hard kiss. Still angry, I went to push him away, but when his tongue entered my mouth, the fire of the fight died in me.

I hungrily met the thrusts of his tongue with my own, wrapping my arms around his neck. He guided me backwards towards what I assumed was his room as he greedily sucked on my lips. After fumbling our way through the dark room, my calves touched the side of his bed, stopping us. He pulled away from me to switch on the lamp.

His shirt was hastily ripped away and my eyes regarded his perfect form. Reaching for my sweater, he swept it off over my head and growled at the view of my breasts through my bra. Leaning over, he gently bit down on a nipple through the lace of it. I moaned and gripped his hair, needing him closer. He nipped at me again, causing me to groan in pleasure.

Standing upright again, he looked down at me with hooded eyes that were full of lust and longing. I was sure my own gaze matched his. We both started undoing our jeans, wrenching them off as quickly as we could. He'd pulled off his boxer briefs as well, but I still stood in my bra and panties. My eyes dropped to his erect cock, which pulsated with need.

"I'm going to fuck you now, Pepper," he told me smugly, and I wanted nothing more than for that to happen. I expected him to tell me to lie down, but he spun me around instead. "Lie down face-first but keep that sexy little ass pointed up. I want to see it while I fuck your pussy from behind."

My body shivered at his erotic command, and I complied willingly. His hands pulled my panties down to about mid-thigh, where he left them, before he slowly dragged his hands up along the sides of my body. It nearly drove me crazy, and I shoved my ass out farther, begging him to touch me more.

I felt a finger slide into my core and whimpered at the surprise intrusion.

"Baby, you're so wet for me. I've barely touched you and I

can see you want me badly. Do you want me like I want you?"

I nodded frantically so he would know how much I wanted him. His finger slipped back out and I whined in frustration.

"If you want me, then no more games, Pepper," he said as his cock, wet with pre-cum, teased my own moist entrance.

I nodded again but moaned when he barely stuck the head in.

"Babe, that's not good enough. I need to hear the words. You belong to me, and I will take good fucking care of you. I'm waiting to hear the words so I can shove my cock into you and give you a hot orgasm. Say it, Pepper. Tell me you want me and that you belong to me."

I tried pushing back towards him so he would push himself all the way in, but he gripped my hips hard with both hands and held me still. He wanted me to tell him that I belonged to him, but I didn't belong to anyone. This was just feeding my weakness.

His hand came around to my front and started taunting my clit with alternating quick and slow movements. It was all so stimulating.

"I want you," I moaned into the duvet as I fisted it with each hand. His cock stayed where it was, tip in and unmoving. And while he teased my clit, I knew he was still waiting.

"Pepper, say the words and I will ram you so hard you'll feel it in your gut. I want your pussy to clench around my cock as your orgasm burns through you. Don't you want that baby?" he crooned.

A hot tear escaped out of my eye. I did want him—so badly. His body was my drug, and I was completely addicted.

"Babe, please. I need you so much. You're everything to me. Why won't you give yourself to me and let me take care of you?" he asked softly as he rocked his tip in and out of me.

"I'm scared of who I will become," I whispered honestly as another tear chased the other one.

"Fuck, Pepper, you're you. Perfect. I hope one day you can trust me."

Without warning, he shoved himself all the way in, and I wailed in pleasure. My orgasm had been waiting by like a crouching tiger, but the moment he'd plowed into me, I'd started to unravel. His finger was still rubbing my clit but had progressed to a faster pace. The electric heat of my orgasm finally surged through my body as he pounded into me. I was so wrapped up in my own pleasure that I hadn't even realized he'd come until I felt it running down my legs.

He pulled out quickly and went to the bathroom. Upon returning, he took a warm rag and cleaned me between my legs. Once he left to return the cloth to the bathroom, I shed the rest of my clothes and climbed under the covers. Still naked, he slid in next to me and pushed his chest against my back. His arm wrapped possessively around me, and we stayed quietly like that for some time.

I could sense that he was upset with me, and suddenly I felt very emotional. Weak. Damn, I hated the feeling, but it was a package deal with Jordan. Without him, I could be tougher, but what was the point? He was protective, intelligent, and sexy as hell. If I pushed him away just to feel solid, it would mean Cole would win in continuing to ruin my life. I was over it. Completely over the way Cole had changed my life. It ended now.

"He doesn't own me anymore. I'm yours if you'll have me," I whispered just loud enough that he could hear me.

His hand guided me over onto my back and he brought his lips to mine, gently kissing me. He ended the kiss so he could look into my eyes, his face serious.

"You'll always be mine, Elizabeth."

Tears rolled down my cheeks at being called my real name. And just like that, it was done. I was Jordan's and he was mine.

Chapter TWENTY-TWO

Jordan

"LOU, DO YOU THINK we could meet up to discuss a few things?" I asked.

Last night had been amazing as Elizabeth and I gave our bodies to one another. And yes, I was fucking calling her by her given name now. We were connecting on such a deep level that I'd never be able to live without her. It had been hard not to stay in bed with her all day, but I still had a company to run. I'd already spent the better part of the morning getting Mr. Cox set up in the conference room with access to all the information he would need.

"Mr. Compton, I don't see what there is to discuss. You still owe me six hundred thousand dollars."

I scowled into the phone. I needed to pull more information from him but he wasn't even going to give me the time of day.

"Lou, please. You obviously had a relationship with my father. Honor your friendship to him by hearing me out."

The sigh on the other line was loud but one that conceded to my request.

"Fine. I have time after a meeting this afternoon. Can you come by around 4:30?" he questioned.

"Certainly. Thanks, Lou." I hung up and checked my emails.

Andi had sent me a few about some customer appointments I had later in the week. She'd already put them on my calendar for me. Then I found one from my Elizabeth and opened it up.

Jordan,

I forgot to tell you that my mother invited you to dinner tonight. My parents live near your mom's house. My mother's a great cook. I'd love for you to come with me. They've never seen me in a relationship. You'd win them over instantly for the pure fact that you were the one to break through to me.

Yours,

Elizabeth

I smiled at her email. Of course I wanted to meet her parents. They needed to know that I cared deeply for their daughter and I wasn't going anywhere. I loved that she'd used her real name to sign the email. It proved that she was serious about trusting me.

Elizabeth,

There's no way I would miss it. I can't wait to dazzle your parents with my charm. Tell them it will be closer to six by the time I get there. I've got a meeting at 4:30, but I'll come just as soon as it's over.

Jordan

Andi walked into my office with a frown on her face and plopped down into the chair in front of me.

"Your brother is so freaking difficult!" she shrieked at me. *Oh boy.*

"What did the prick do now?" I questioned. Those two had some serious issues that always threatened to tear them apart, but then miraculously they would be in love again. They were extremely confusing to any outsiders.

"He has a surprise for my birthday tomorrow. I told him not to buy me anything, but he's acting really secretive, which means he's hiding something big. Every time I try to ask him about it, he just smiles at me innocently. Jordan, you need to find out what he's doing and tell him to cut it out," she huffed out at me.

Yep. Those two were completely dramatic.

"Andi, who cares if he does something for you? You're his girlfriend and he loves you. Don't you think you're being kind of snotty about it?"

"Jordan Compton! I am not being a snot! Your brother just acts irrationally, and I'm afraid he'll do something outrageous and expensive. Just tell him I want a low-key birthday tomorrow."

"Fine, I'll tell him, but he never listens to me. You were warned. Can you tell me Eliz—er—Pepper's parents' address? I'm meeting her there for dinner tonight."

Her eyes widened and her sour mood dissipated. A grin broke out over her face.

"Shit, Jordan! You about called her Elizabeth! Nobody calls her that. The fact she even told you her name means the girl is in love with you. Here, I'll write it down for you." She happily jotted down the address and skipped out of my office.

That girl was just as crazy as Jackson.

Mr. Cox, who now insisted that I call him AJ because he was close to my age and it just felt weird, prepped me for my meeting. My attorney couldn't meet with us on such short notice and tried to talk me out of going, but I wouldn't hear of it. When I walked into the conference room, Lou and his attorney sat stone-faced as they waited for me.

"Mr. Compton," Lou acknowledged, and his attorney nodded his head at me.

"So what is it that you've thought it necessary to bring us in for an impromptu meeting?" Lou's attorney asked, cutting right to the chase. This guy was such a dick.

"Sir," I began, but he cut me off.

"Call me Calvin."

"Calvin, I'm having trouble locating the money. I wanted to ask if there was any way we could push back the date. I've given you half of the money as a token of good faith. Certainly, businessmen like yourselves can understand the need to want to find the funds properly and not wipe out your working capital."

"Mr. Compton," Calvin interrupted, "we already discussed a deadline and we're going to have to stick to that. Lou has some prior commitments that cannot be broken."

Ignoring Calvin, I figured I would hurry and try to pull information out of Lou.

"Lou, who was the unnamed partner? Please, it would help me out."

Lou sighed, and Calvin just rolled his eyes at my questioning.

"Surely you know that it was Nadia Compton. She and your father seemed to be really close even though I believe she is married to your brother. The woman is shrewd in her business dealings, not one I would want to cross."

My teeth clenched in anger. I had known she'd been involved by seeing the checks, but it still pissed me off to hear it.

"I thought you didn't deal in illegal activities, Lou," I stated, probing him.

"Son, I have never dealt in anything illegal. Now, I am sorry if your father and quite possibly Nadia were involved in something fraudulent, but I assure you, I was not. They presented an opportunity to me in the most professional way. I am due my cut and I expect it by the end of our prior agreement."

"First of all, Lou, I am not your son. Second, I don't know how you can turn a blind eye to all of this! I can smell something fishy and I just came into this mess!" I was furious now at his ignorance.

Calvin stood up and walked over to me. "Mr. Compton, I think it's time you leave."

Standing quickly, I faced Calvin. "You both can plead ignorance, but if there is anything illegal going on, you both could be implicated!" I shouted in Calvin's face. His face was turning red, and I knew he was getting pissed.

"Your fucking father was a sorry-ass motherfucker that my friend and client somehow got involved with. Do not come in here and attempt to threaten either one of us. My client is innocent of any illegal activity. You need to leave, little boy, and go finish running your legacy into the ground. Your incompetent father gave you a head start."

Before he could even finish, I popped him in the nose with my fist. It happened before I could stop it, and blood gushed immediately, soaking his shirt. His red face was mixed with anger and shock, but he made no moves to hit me back.

Lou's voice boomed over at me, reminding me of my father. "Jordan, get out of here before I call the police. There will be no more 'meetings.' Only you depositing the money. End of discussion. Out!" he roared.

I glared at Calvin and then stalked out of the room.

Chapter
TWENTY-THREE

Elizabeth

"WHAT ABOUT THIS ONE?" my mother asked, holding up a pearl necklace. I held it up to me so I could see it in the mirror. The dress was at the apartment, but I remembered how low the neckline was on it.

"Nah, it doesn't go with the whole 'red dress' look. I need something sexier." She nodded her agreement and continued to peruse the pile on the bed.

"Ah, here you go. This is gorgeous," she exclaimed, smiling, holding up rather large teardrop diamond necklace. It was beautiful and would go perfectly with the dress. I took it from her to look at it closer.

"Mom, it's exquisite. I think this is the one. Do you have earrings and a bracelet to match?" I asked, clasping it around my neck so I could admire it in the mirror.

She handed them over so I could try them on. "Honey, I feel like we're dressing you up for the prom you never attended. I can't help but feel ecstatic over this gala. Your father and I look forward to meeting your boyfriend. The relief on your dad's face was evident when I told him you had a love interest. He's always worried that you would have been too jaded to ever successfully have any future relationships after what that jerk did to you." Her eyes were teary, and my own misted over as well.

"Mom, he's wonderful. You are going to love him. He adores his family, he's successful, and he is drop-dead gorgeous. I'm still amazed at how much he likes me," I admitted honestly.

"Sweetie, you are beautiful and intelligent. Any man would be lucky to have you." I grinned at her and took the jewelry off.

When the doorbell rang, we both shrieked like teenage girls, running for the door. I opened the door to a brooding Jordan. After he saw me, his face morphed into a grin.

"Hey, babe," he greeted, embracing me.

"Hi, Jordan. Meet my mother, Sandra." I gestured to her. She grinned as she held out her hand for him to shake. Instead, he brought her in for a quick hug, and I swear she blushed.

"Nice to meet you, Sandra. I got these for you."

She gasped when he handed her the box of Godiva chocolates. I just rolled my eyes. He knew the way to a woman's heart.

"Why, Jordan, how adorably sweet of you. Thank you for the chocolates. We can certainly enjoy these after dinner with some wine." Smiling, she walked back towards the kitchen to check on the lasagna.

"I missed you." He chastely kissed me on the lips.

"I missed you too, Jordan. Daddy is running a few minutes late. Something came up at work. He'll be here soon."

He kissed me again, this time deeper. I sighed as my body involuntarily ignited at his touch. Finally, he withdrew and smiled at me.

"You better cut that out. Otherwise, we'll never make it to dinner, babe, and that won't make a good impression on your folks."

I sighed again but grinned back at him. "Fine, but I can't promise I'll be able to control myself in the car on the way back home," I teased. "I took a cab so we could ride back together." Grabbing his hand, I dragged him into the kitchen.

"Dinner is about ready, guys. Your daddy is almost home. He just texted me. Why don't we enjoy some wine while we wait?" She poured three glasses for us, and we chatted easily while we waited for him.

Jordan, ever the charmer, had Mom eating out of his hand by the time I heard Daddy enter the kitchen. She had resorted to call-ing him Jordie, making my heart swell inside.

"Darling, I'm so sorry I am late. I got caught up with some hothead asshole," he grumbled as he leaned over to kiss my moth-er's cheek.

Jordan visibly tensed at my father's words, and I sent him a worried glance.

"Honey, what happened to your nose?" my mother shrieked.

Daddy's nose was swollen and his eyes were turning black underneath.

"Don't worry about it. We've got a guest. Hi, I'm Calvin Jones."

When he turned to introduce himself to Jordan, his face turned bright red with fury.

"Fucking Jordan Compton!" he shouted, causing me and Mom to jump.

What the hell is going on with these two?

"You've got to be kidding me," Jordan muttered under his breath.

"Daddy, what's going on?" I asked, grabbing Jordan's hand.

"Your *boyfriend* punched me in the nose!" he yelled over at me. Daddy never got this upset, but he was seething with anger. This dinner was turning to shit really fast.

"Now, Calvin, calm down. I don't know what's going on with you two, but Jordan is a nice young man. And I hate to remind you, but he is also your daughter's boyfriend," Mom told him calmly.

Daddy was having a hard time keeping his cool. Jordan was tense beside me, ready to snap. He was also never like this. I couldn't understand the whole situation.

"Daddy, I don't understand. Why would Jordan punch you? How do you two know each other?" I questioned, concern lacing my voice. This was not how this meeting was supposed to go down.

Jordan spoke up before Daddy could. "Your *daddy* represents the man that's trying to take money from my company. He called my father incompetent and insulted my ability run my business," he fumed.

My mouth dropped open as I realized what had happened.

"Get out of my fucking house," Daddy ordered nastily, glaring at Jordan.

"Calvin! Absolutely not. You both need to chill out!" my mother shouted at Daddy. Your daughter is dating him, and I suggest you learn to deal with it if you don't want to hurt her." His jaw was visibly clenching and unclenching as he considered Mom's words.

"I'll be waiting at the dinner table," Daddy uttered coldly as he stormed into the dining room, Mom on his heels. Jordan sighed in relief once he'd left the room.

"You punched my daddy?" I hissed at him.

His features softened when he looked at me. "Babe, he got in my face and insulted my father. It was instinct. I felt horrible after I did it. I'm so sorry. That was completely out of character for me. This fucking sucks." He ran his hands through his hair. I could tell he was really upset over the whole ordeal.

"Come here. We'll figure it out. Just make it through dinner, Jordan. I'm sure Daddy will cool off." I smiled at him and pecked his lips. He didn't look convinced but nodded anyway.

We made our way to the dining room and Mom patted my Daddy on the shoulder before returning to the kitchen to retrieve the lasagna.

"Darling, how is the gala coming along?" Daddy asked, not looking over at Jordan as we took our seats.

"Daddy, it's going great. Stan and I have been working end-lessly to pull everything together, but I am pleased to say that everything is a go. I'm looking forward to showing him my abilities on my first big event. He said that if I prove myself, I'll be able to handle the entire thing next year. I'm terribly excited!" I beamed, hoping he would get past the whole Jordan thing.

His smile was genuine, letting me know that he was trying. "Princess, that's wonderful! I am so happy for you. It really seems like your life is just the way you want it." Daddy was trying to be the bigger man, which made me incredibly pleased.

"Yes, Daddy. I am excited about the gala. There are going to be hundreds of influential people there. It will be an exciting time for me." I grinned at him, trying to lighten the mood.

Jordan sat silently beside me. He too was trying for me. These guys really cared for me, and it made my heart hurt that they already hated each other.

Mom brought out the lasagna in one hand and the salad in the other. She was smiling her fake entertaining smile. I felt bad for her and threw her a look of encouragement.

"Dinner is served, everyone. Please enjoy," she said breezily. We all took turns putting portions of food on our plates. Mom poured Daddy a glass of wine as well and set the bottle down in front of her. It would definitely be one of those nights.

"Sandra, this lasagna is delicious. You are quite the cook," Jordan complimented, smiling at her.

She chuckled at him. "Thank you, Jordie! It was my mother's

recipe. I've spent the better part of thirty years perfecting it," she explained, blushing.

Daddy frowned, which made me cringe.

Daddy and Jordan were making a point not to look at each other or talk to each other. That meant that the attention was brought upon me and Mom.

"Daddy, I need to tell you something," I revealed, growing serious. "I was mugged Sunday night and I think it was Cole," I confessed.

His face turned red with fury again, but this time it was directed at Cole. "What the hell, Pepper? Why didn't you say anything?" he bellowed.

"Her name is Elizabeth," Jordan growled from beside me, shocking both me and Daddy.

"Excuse me?" Daddy asked.

"I said, her name is Elizabeth. That dickhead gave her that name. Don't encourage it." His glare met Daddy's, and I shifted nervously in my seat.

Mom quietly ate her lasagna, trying to stay out of the argument. Daddy stared at Jordan, mouth gaping.

"You're right. I'm so sorry, Elizabeth. Now tell me why in the hell you didn't tell me this the moment it happened!"

"Daddy, I didn't want to worry you. I wasn't hurt. He held a gun to Jordan's head and demanded my purse." Daddy smirked when I said the part about Jordan and tears filled my eyes. I could tell he instantly regretted it.

"Elizabeth, I'm sorry."

I blinked back the tears and tried to focus on eating my lasagna. Jordan reached over and grabbed my hand, squeezing it.

"It's okay, Daddy. I'm just bummed. He knows where I live now," I told him as my chin quivered.

"He won't touch you. I'll kill him," Jordan promised.

The look of surprise on my Daddy's face made my heart swell. Maybe they could learn to get along for my sake. Jordan gently kissed my cheek and went back to eating his lasagna. When I looked up at Daddy again, he was looking at Jordan, his mouth open.

"Jordan, keep my Elizabeth safe," Daddy said to him.

Jordan looked back at him with confidence in his eyes. "Sir, I will fucking choke the life out of him if he even looks at her."

And for the first time that evening, Daddy smiled at him.

Chapter TWENTY-FOUR

Jordan

THE RIDE HOME was quiet. I still could not believe that Elizabeth's dad was fucking Calvin. *Unbelievable.*

"Want to go to your place or mine?" I asked her on the way back.

"Mine," she replied quietly. She was clearly upset over the entire ordeal.

Calvin and I had managed to respect her and not fight with each other through the dinner. We hadn't stuck around afterwards and were already heading back home.

"Elizabeth, I'm so sorry. I've never been one to result to violence, but he fucking pissed me off when he insulted my dad. I saw red and acted before I realized that it was a terrible idea. Please forgive me, baby." I wanted her to know that I wasn't some meathead who went around punching people when I got angry.

"It's okay," she answered softly.

Once we arrived at her apartment, I turned off the car.

"Babe, can I come up?" I hoped she would agree.

"Jordan, of course you can."

We quietly got out and made it upstairs to her apartment without incident.

"Hey, guys!" Olive chirped from her position on the arm of the couch. Every time I saw that girl, she was sitting like a cat perched on a limb of a tree, long legs twisted underneath her in what looked to be an uncomfortable position.

"Hi, Olive," we said in unison. Elizabeth went over to her and hugged her. I sat in the recliner and started texting Jackson the story about tonight's events with Calvin.

"Olive? Did you have a chance to call the bakery today?" Elizabeth questioned.

"Yes, and I also put in our catering order at Andi's favorite restaurant. I still feel bad that she's having her party here all because of me. Pepper, I would have tried to go out for her, you know." Her eyes filled with tears.

"Sweetie, I know you would, but Andi loves you too much to make you feel uncomfortable. We're going to have a blast. I'm going to head to the liquor store tomorrow on the way home from work. The decorations are in my closet. Is she staying with Jackson tonight?"

"Yeah, babe. I'm texting Jackson right now. She'll come back here after work tomorrow for the party," I told her.

"Great. That will give us time to decorate. Olive, come help me get all of the decorations out."

The girls disappeared into her room. My phone chimed again.

Jackie: No fucking way dude. That has to be the worst possible scenario. So I'm assuming you didn't find out anything at the meeting since you punched Calvin?

Me: Well, he just told me what we already knew. They claim no illegal involvement and Nadia is right smack in the middle. How is the divorce coming along?

Jackie: I hope the bitch goes down. Joel finally convinced her to sign the divorce papers and we'll be finalized in the coming weeks. I can't fucking wait to get that monkey off my back so I can move on with my life. Andi deserves it.

Me: I agree. Congrats dude. Oh, speaking of Andi, she doesn't want you to go overboard for her birthday.

Jackie: Ha. Not going to happen.

Me: I tried. Talk to you tomorrow.

"Get your lazy ass over here and help us hang these streamers," Elizabeth barked from the stool she was standing on. I laughed because, even on the barstool, she couldn't reach the high ceilings.

I strode over and let her boss me around for the next hour while we decorated. She thrived on being in control in situations like this. Grinning at her the entire time, I did as I was told. After we'd decorated, we retired to her room.

"I'm going to hop in the shower," she told me as she shed her clothes on the way to the bathroom. Catching a glimpse of her perfect ass as she shimmied out of her jeans, I quickly followed suit. By the time I was undressed, she'd already stepped into the steamy shower.

Climbing inside with her, I took a moment to observe her as she washed her hair. With the water running over her skin and her breasts pointed out as she tilted her hair back to rinse her hair, I felt my dick harden at the beautiful sight. I wouldn't ever get enough of her. Reaching out for her, I gently cupped her breasts in my hands. Her head tilted back down and she met my heated gaze. The smile she gave me made my chest constrict. She was absolutely exquisite. I was a lucky man.

"Jordan, you look pretty hot with water running over your chest," she pronounced sweetly as her fingers delicately skirted across my abs.

"Babe, I was thinking the same damn thing about you," I confessed. My mouth descended upon hers and we kissed hard, all sweetness gone.

Her moan into my mouth was carnal. We wanted each other right then. I grabbed her ass and hoisted her up. She wrapped legs around my hips and her arms around my neck, catching my drift. Turning, I pressed her against the cold tile, and she yelped from the feel of it against her hot skin.

Slowly, I eased her onto my shaft, and she tossed her head back in pleasure. She was already wet for me. It would seem I had that effect on her. Once she was situated, I plunged in and out of her as her pussy gripped my dick. Her neck was exposed to me so I sucked and nibbled her while she bounced on my cock. She moaned loudly, indicating that she was close to her orgasm. In the next instant, I felt the walls of her sex constrict my cock as her climax tore through her. Immediately after hers, I lost it and my hot come burst into her.

"Will making love with you ever get old?" she asked, cheeks flushed.

I chastely kissed her lips before replying. "Never. We were made for each other."

Her smile was my undoing, and I spent the rest of the night showing her exactly what a perfect fit we were.

Chapter TWENTY-FIVE

Elizabeth

LAST NIGHT HAD BEEN perfect. *Can I get away with staying in bed with him for the rest of my life?* For as much as we'd made love, I was sore but still wanted more, completely addicted to his body.

Work went by in a flash as Stan and I prepared for the gala tomorrow night. I'd received my phone finally and was ecstatic to once again have a better connection to Jordan. When five rolled around, I was eager to get home to prepare for Andi's party.

Jordan had been busy working with the fraud examiner all day, so his texts had been short, one-word replies. Before I left, I figured I would do something to get his blood flowing. Glad that my office door was closed, I shimmied my skirt up over my knees to above my thighs, revealing my pink panties and thinking that Andi would be proud of what I was about to do.

I snapped the picture and texted it to him. His response was immediate.

Jordan: BABE! You're KILLING me right now. I've got a hard-on because of your sexy ass picture and AJ's sitting across the table from me!

I laughed. No more one-word answers for Jordan. Taking it up another notch, I slid my panties over and slipped a finger into my wet folds. Positioning the phone with my other hand, I took another picture and texted it to him.

Jordan: Fuck me.

When my phone started ringing, I smiled.

"Hi, Jordan. How's your day?" I asked nonchalantly, knowing that he was going crazy.

He didn't buy into it and cut straight to the chase. "Babe, how does your finger feel inside of you? Do you wish it were my finger?" he whispered into the phone. Things suddenly went from joking to hot.

"It feels good but yours feels better."

"Slide another one in and close your eyes. I'm touching you. Can you feel me?"

My eyes fluttered closed as I imagined his fingers in me. My breath hitched at the visual.

"That's it, baby. Curl your fingers. Do you feel your g-spot?" he crooned into the phone.

I did as I was told and gasped. "Yes, Jordan. I feel it. Oh my God," I moaned back at him.

His growl did me in, and I almost dropped the phone. My orgasm racked through me, and I could feel my pussy clenching around my fingers.

"Is everything okay?" Stan questioned, bursting into the room.

Shit! I guessed I had been a little loud. Jerking out my fingers, I fumbled to pull my skirt back down. Stan was just staring, open-mouthed, making no moves to leave my office. My face burned with embarrassment.

"Who the hell is that?" Jordan barked into the phone.

"My boss, Stan. I need to go." He was still griping when I hung up on him.

"Uh, Stan, I…" I tried to explain, stammering.

He face morphed from shock to a huge smile. "No need to explain, Pepper. Next time though, let me take care of it for you. I'd do anything to see that look on your face again." He grinned once more and left my office.

This had to be the most embarrassing thing that had ever happened to me. What was worse than his just walking in was the fact that he'd offered to do it for me next time. Jordan was going to shit a brick when I told him. If I even told him.

"Just put it over here," I ordered Bray as he walked in with a present for Andi. We didn't have the best relationship but I was trying for Andi's sake since her shrink said that we all needed to accept him into our group to help her fully heal. Olive rounded the corner, and Bray did what every guy does when they see Olive. He drank her up. His eyes were about to pop out of his head.

"Put your tongue back in your mouth, asswipe," I snapped at him, rolling my eyes.

Collecting himself, he grinned at her. "Nice to meet you. I'm Bray."

She gave him her fake smile but didn't extend her hand to meet his. His frown made me laugh. Olive was loyal as hell to us, and she hated all of the stories I'd told her regarding Andi's past with Bray.

"You too," she said and retreated back into the kitchen.

"I'll never live it down, will I?" he asked rhetorically as he headed to the table where the other presents were.

Ignoring him, I answered anyway. "Nope, dickhead. So don't get any ideas about Olive. If you ever cared about Andi, don't go there." He glared at me but nodded his head. I loved being a bitch to him. It somehow made up for what he had done to Andi. *Almost.*

The doorbell rang and I hurried over to answer it. After grabbing the bags of food and paying the delivery guy, I brought them to the kitchen. Bray was leaning against the counter, smiling over at Olive, who was blushing. Her light chocolate skin would burn red around her cheeks and neck when was embarrassed.

"Make yourself useful and help me put out all of the food," I demanded in Bray's direction. The three of us were putting out the food when I heard the door open.

Jordan suddenly appeared in the kitchen. His eyes were on fire when he saw me. He stalked over to me, looped his arms around my waist, and tossed me over his shoulder.

"Jordan! Cut it out!" I shrieked as he tore off to my bedroom.

Slamming the door behind him, he set me back down.

"What's your deal?" I asked angrily.

"Nobody is allowed to see what's mine," he growled, grasping my face in his hands. Possessive Jordan was pretty hot.

His lips pressed to mine and we kissed fiercely. I wanted to convey how much I was his with my tongue. Understanding my message, one of his hands slid under the waistband of my skirt and panties right to my clit.

"Oh God, Jordan," I moaned into his mouth. He rubbed at a furious rate, and before I knew it, I was crying out his name again as an orgasm ripped through me.

Quickly, he pulled away and grinned at me.

"Mine," he declared, eyes flicking down to my skirt. Turning on his heels, he left me in my room panting.

Chapter TWENTY-SIX

Jordan

I HAD SEEN RED when I heard Stan's voice on the other end of Elizabeth's phone while she had been pleasuring herself. When she hung up on me, I'd nearly lost it. In her bedroom, I reminded her who she belonged to, and she didn't seem to complain.

Watching her reenter the kitchen looking flushed had me grinning. She was beautiful when she had that post-orgasmic glow. When her eyes met mine, she smiled shyly. Our exchange was interrupted when Andi and Jackson walked in.

"Happy birthday!" Elizabeth and Olive shrieked as they ran over to hug her.

"Thanks, girls! Everything looks lovely. I'm so happy!" she squealed.

As the girls chattered happily about whatever it was girls talked about, Jackson walked over to me and Bray.

"You guys want a drink?" he asked us. We both nodded and he poured us both a Jack and Coke.

"How come you guys never told me that Andi and Pepper's roommate Olive was a freaking goddess?" Bray asked, glancing over at her. I grinned at him, but Jackson was scowling. No surprise there.

"Bray, leave her the fuck alone. She's a fragile girl, and you tend to leave a path of destruction wherever you go," Jackson spat at him. *Oh shit. Not again.*

"What the fuck is everyone's problem? Did you and Pepper place bets on who could be the biggest ass to me?" he huffed angrily. These guys were impossible.

"You two need to chill out before Andi gets pissed. Let's eat," I ordered as the girls came into the kitchen.

We all enjoyed our dinner and talked easily. As much as everyone hated the idea of Bray liking Olive, I thought it would be kind of cool if we all could hang out like this more often. Olive didn't look innocent about the whole thing as she kept stealing glances at him. The energy between them was charged, even if nobody else wanted to admit it. I had a feeling Elizabeth and Jackson would be pissed at where I could see this going.

"Oh my God, this cake is so good," Andi moaned as she ate her chocolate birthday cake. Jackson couldn't take his eyes off of her lips, and I chuckled. Those two were something else.

Elizabeth took my hand and winked at me.

"Okay, Andi, you better quit making love to your cake. Jackie Boy is getting jealous," Elizabeth teased her. Jackson just shot her a mean look.

"Are you guys ready for presents?" Olive asked suddenly, jerking up from her chair. She looked incredibly uncomfortable and ready to escape her seat beside Bray. His shit-eating grin told me he was up to no good.

We all refreshed our drinks and headed into the living room. Andi sat in Jackson's lap on the recliner while Bray and Olive sat on opposite ends of the couch. Elizabeth sidled up next to me on the loveseat.

Andi picked up a bag from the coffee table.

"Let's see... This is from Olive," she told us as she opened it.

She squealed when she pulled out a pair of dangly earrings and a matching necklace. "I love them, Olive. Thank you."

Olive smiled back at her. I noticed that Bray had sneakily moved closer to her on the couch, and I bit back a laugh.

"This one is from Bray," Andi announced as she opened up her next gift.

Inside was a Yankees sweatshirt and six tickets tucked into it for the first game of the season. Jackson practically threw her off his lap to look at them.

"Bray! You shouldn't have! These probably cost a fortune. I am excited though. It will be so much fun for the six of us to go," she sang excitedly.

He grinned at her, pleased at her happiness with his gift.

"Okay, let's see. The next one is from Jordan." She grinned when she opened my present.

I'd bought her a pink iPod for when she went running with Jackson. There were already a bunch of girly songs on it that I had downloaded for her.

"Jordan, I love it! Thank you so much," she smiled over at me.

Elizabeth squeezed my hand, letting me know that she was pleased with my gift.

"Okay, this one is from Pepper," she said suspiciously as she pulled tissue out of the large Victoria's Secret bag.

Inside, it was stuffed completely full of panties. Everyone roared with laughter because it was no secret that Andi had failed to wear them on numerous occasions.

"Pepper, you're such a bitch! But they're all so pretty so I guess I'll forgive you."

They blew kisses at each other.

"Okay, the last bag must be from Jackson!" she exclaimed, kissing his cheek. When she opened it, her eyes filled with tears.

It was a very expensive camera. Now she'd be able to take

some pretty badass pictures of her buildings with that thing. She wrapped her arms around his neck, and he nuzzled her breasts. Those two never heard of such a thing called too much PDA.

"I have one more thing for you," he revealed, handing her an envelope from his jacket pocket.

She frowned at the envelope, and I laughed. Shooting me a glare, she opened it. Inside were two airline tickets to Paris. He was in trouble.

"Jackson! You promised not to go overboard. These were probably very expensive," she chided.

He just gave her a smug smile. "You're worth it, Andi. I told you I was going to get you whatever I wanted. The trip isn't until January. You have plenty of time to get over it."

She rolled her eyes but kissed him again.

"Thank you, everyone. I love all of it. Now let's get drunk!"

Several hours later, everyone was getting borderline wasted.

"It's called 'Wrong,'" I told them, once again explaining the rules. After many failed attempts of trying to learn the game that clearly only Elizabeth and I had mastered, we finally gave up and just took shots for the fun of it.

Jackson, in the middle of Andi's giggling, scooped her up and hauled her to the bedroom. I laughed at them. Elizabeth had moved her legs into my lap, and I stroked them underneath her skirt while she chattered on about an exhibit she was excited to unveil at the gala.

My eyes flitted over to Bray and Olive. He was right up against her, whispering into her ear. Her eyes were closed, but she was smiling. I watched his pinky stroke the outside of her thigh, and she shivered. When he sucked on her earlobe, she moaned.

They were completely oblivious to us. Elizabeth, unaware of what was going on, kept on talking. I decided I wasn't one to cock block and stood up with her in my arms.

"God, it's so hot when you pick me up. You're such a man," she purred.

I chuckled at her words. "I'm about to show you exactly how manly I am," I said confidently, carrying her into the bedroom.

Chapter TWENTY-SEVEN

Elizabeth

MY HEAD POUNDED in conjunction with my ringing alarm clock. Jordan's naked body was draped heavily over me. His soft snoring was adorable, and I bit back a laugh so I wouldn't wake him. Slowly, I eased out from underneath him, but his arm grabbed my hip and pulled me back over.

"Where do you think you're going?" he asked, voice gravelly with sleep.

"Some of us have work to do today," I teased. His hand slipped down to my lower body and I gasped.

"Make love with me before we have to get up," he commanded sweetly.

Pushing him over, I straddled his stomach. "I think we have enough time for that," I grinned and eased myself down over his now hard cock. One of his hands grabbed a breast while his other hand slipped down to my clit. He groaned as I rode him slowly. His hand dropped from my breast to my hip and urged me to go faster. Complying, I sped up my bouncing and whimpered as I felt my orgasm getting close.

"That's it, babe. Come for me. I want to see your beautiful face when you cry out my name." His thumb and finger softly pinched my clit and my body convulsed as my climax took over.

"Jordan, oh my God," I breathed as my body kept clenching around him with my aftershocks. Soon after, his own release pumped into me, and I collapsed onto his chest.

His hands softly rubbed my back, and I would have been happy staying conjoined like that for the rest of my life.

"I think we need to move that table back a few feet from that exhibit. Don't you think the exhibit needs to be the centerpiece, not the ice sculpture on the food table?" I asked Stan. It was completely weird being around him today after yesterday's embarrassing event, but I had no choice. I chose to ignore that it had ever happened and proceed like normal.

"You're right. Let's move it over about six more feet," he agreed.

We each grabbed an end and repositioned it farther down. Satisfied, we went back into Stan's office to discuss the timeline of events that were to happen tonight.

"Once the guests arrive, we'll open up the silent auction for them to come in and view the items. The bar will be open and the waitstaff will walk around serving hors d'oeuvres to our guests. At the end of the first hour, Mr. Callahan will make a toast and announce our sponsors. I would like our main sponsor to say a few words, and then we can open the buffet. After everyone's finished, we'll have a cocktail hour for everyone to mingle and view the exhibits. At the end of that hour, we'll have Mr. Callahan speak on behalf of the museum to thank everyone for coming. After that, we will close out the silent auction and notify the winners."

"Okay, Stan. So where exactly do you want me during all of this?" I questioned.

"Well, I think you might do well to schmooze with the guests. A pretty girl like yourself will make them feel welcome. Are you still leaving at three to get ready?"

"Uh, yes. Okay, I will greet the guests and make sure they are enjoying themselves."

"Pepper, you can go ahead and go. It's close to three and everything is set up and ready. I will stay and let in the caterers and support staff. Get here about six thirty so we can iron down anything before the guests arrive at seven."

I nodded and left quickly before he could say anything more about my looks. It was evident that Stan suddenly had a newfound infatuation with me, and it was getting to be quite annoying. He'd never showed any real interest until Jordan had walked into the picture. Men were difficult creatures.

When I arrived back at the apartment, there was an envelope propped up against the door. Picking it up, I realized it was addressed to me. After reading the note, I suddenly felt ill.

Peppermint Pussy,

I see you're doing well for yourself. You've gone on to have a successful career while some of us have nothing. Maybe I should finish what I started all those years ago. Enjoy the gala.

C

Well this sucked. Not only had he decided to threaten me, but he also knew my schedule. Letting myself inside, I slammed the door behind me.

Chapter
TWENTY-EIGHT

Jordan

"JORDAN, YOU NEED to see this," AJ said from across the table.

I got up and walked over to him.

"Have you heard of Aidan Holdings?" he questioned.

I shook my head, wondering where he was going with this.

"Well, apparently Aidan Holdings, which I can only assume spells Nadia backwards, was opened up about a year ago as a subsidiary of Compton Enterprises. The documentation on this account is vague at best. From what I can see, there were multiple deposits each month from several different companies. I am assuming they are investors into this Aidan Holdings. It seems that every so often Aidan Holdings will pay out to a particular company a little over what they originally invested, and then you see a blast of deposits right after from new companies that hadn't previously paid in. I'm guessing they are using these payouts to prove to new companies why they should invest. It appears that Aidan Holdings is robbing Paul to pay Peter. Then, they are showing deposits into both your and Jackson's trust as employee bonuses. Afterwards, they take part of the money and send the check to the original investor. The excess seems to be getting wired into an offshore account called NC Limited. Jordan, I feel like I've only scratched the surface, but I think this is huge. As unfortunate as it is, I believe Lou Jennings was a pawn in this scheme. He is clearly one of the many investors awaiting their payouts. With your dad's death, it would appear that things are starting to unravel. She's clearly having trouble keeping it up by herself."

I couldn't believe how big this whole thing was turning out to be. This couldn't be good for our company's future.

"So what do we do, AJ? Do we call the IRS? The SEC? What about Nadia's involvement?" I demanded, frantic for answers.

"Calm down, Jordan. I've got a call in to my good friend Pete at the SEC. He'll tell us how to proceed. In the meantime, don't let Nadia know that we are onto her. If we can get past their divorce, then things won't be as complicated when it hits the fan. All of this will eventually come to a head and your company will receive some negative publicity. I'm hoping that, by us bringing it to the SEC, we're showing good faith that we've identified the fraud and will do whatever means necessary to correct it. You and Jackson are innocent, and so is Lou Jennings for that matter. Unfortunately, you will all suffer in some way because of this. How much will depend on what we uncover."

I sighed and rubbed my face in frustration. Dad had really left us with a big mess. It seemed so uncharacteristically like him. If I had to guess, Nadia had somehow manipulated him into getting involved in this scheme. The woman was a viper and I questioned to this day why my brother had even married her.

"Okay, AJ. I will keep a lid on it. Just let me know if you need anything else from me. What should we do about Lou? He's going to demand his money pretty soon, and we can't give it to him until we figure everything out."

"Jordan, we need to have a meeting with Lou and his attorney. I bet that they will want to cooperate with us once they find out that the SEC will be getting involved. Lou runs an empire himself. He isn't going to want this to ruin what he has worked so hard to build. We'll meet with them tomorrow, and by then I'll know more from my friend at the SEC. Hang in there, Jordan. We're going to figure this out."

"I'll set it up. It might be a little difficult though. I sort of punched Lou's attorney yesterday. And then I discovered I'm dating his daughter. Let's just say it was an awkward dinner last night."

AJ roared with laughter until tears rolled down his cheeks. "Damn Jordan! It's pretty boring most days doing my job, but that right there is entertainment. Get the appointment set up. Grovel if you have to. It'll be harder than hell keeping a straight face at that meeting."

"Thanks for the support, AJ," I replied, rolling my eyes at him.

After he left, I shot Elizabeth a text.

Me: Wish me luck. I'm about to call Lou and beg him and your dad for another appointment. AJ found some interesting information. I'll fill you in later. Miss you.

Elizabeth: Cole left a note on my door today.

Me: What the hell? What did it say?

Elizabeth: Basically that he knows my schedule and wouldn't mind finishing what he started long ago.

This guy was psychotic, and it made me nervous that he was threatening her at her home.

Me: I'm coming over.

Elizabeth: No! Andi just got here and she's going to help me get ready for the gala. I'll be fine, I promise. After the gala, we can leave together so I will be safe then. Call and make your appointment. I'll see you at seven.

Damn, she was so stubborn. If I ran into that guy, I was going to hurt him. But the fact that I knew he had a gun made me sick to my stomach. I needed to look into getting my own very soon.

Chapter TWENTY-NINE

Elizabeth

"SIT STILL, PEPPER," Andi chided, yanking on my hair. She was getting a little too into this whole dress up thing.

"I would have figured you would have wanted to leave my hair down. That's all I ever hear you say anyway. Why did you want to put it up just like I wear it every day?" I asked. We were sitting at the kitchen table so I didn't have access to a mirror, but it felt like she was giving me the same hairstyle as usual but with a few more bobby pins.

"Pepper, I can assure you that your hair does not look like it normally does. You're going to a black-tie event, which means your hair will look best pulled up. When I finish with you, nobody is going to recognize you."

I'd already put in my contacts, which I owned for the rare occasion when I didn't want to wear my glasses. This usually was reserved for swimming and summertime. That in itself would make me look completely different.

Andi went to work on my makeup while I thought about tonight. This whole thing with Cole stressed me out, as if my first gala weren't stressful enough. I had no idea what to expect out of him, but he seemed dead set in ruining me. Considering that I knew he had a gun, it scared the hell out of me.

"What's wrong, Pepper?" Andi asked as she finished with a light coat of lip gloss.

"What? Nothing," I lied as I attempted to avoid her penetrating gaze.

"I'm your best friend and I'm insulted that you would lie to me. I can read when something's wrong. If you were nervous about the gala, you would tell me. Whatever it is that's bothering you, you're trying to keep to yourself."

I sighed and looked up at her, which was not a good idea. My eyes started to mist over. I sighed again in resignation.

"So you know how I was mugged the other day? I think it was someone I knew from my past. Did I ever tell you how I came to get my nickname?"

The frown on her face made me feel guilty for never telling her. I bit back my nervousness and spent the next half hour rehashing every detail. By the end, my tears had thoroughly ruined my makeup, and Andi's face didn't look any better.

"Okay, time to dry up. I'm fixing you up for good, so no more crying. I love you, Elizabeth," she told me, nervously trying out my real name. I smiled at her so she would know I was okay with it.

"Fine, I'm dry. Make me pretty enough to drive Jordan crazy. He drives me nuts most days with his perfect body and annoyingly beautiful smile." I feigned irritation, and she giggled.

"Honey, his jaw will be on the floor the entire night along with every other male in the place."

She finally finished and we went to my room so I could put the dress on.

Slipping the red, shiny material over my body, I instantly felt sexy. My red lace bra and thong were going to be a hit too later tonight when Jordan took off my dress. Andi handed me a pair of her "fuck me" heels. I slid them on and put on my mother's jewelry.

"Okay, let's go take a look in the big-ass mirror in your room," I suggested, turning to face her. Her eyes were bugging out of her head, immediately making me feel embarrassed. "What is it, Andi? Does it look bad?" I questioned, worry lacing my voice.

"Hell no, Pep—Elizabeth! You are going to be every man's wet dream. Even Jackson and Bray would be having dirty thoughts about you right now. You look breathtakingly beautiful," she praised as she eyeballed me.

"Gross! Thank God I won't be seeing those two goobers tonight," I teased, making a sour face at her. She grabbed my hand and dragged me into her room.

When I stepped up to the mirror, my lips parted as I took in the sight. The woman who looked back at me was radiant. Her hair was swept delicately up into a chignon with loose tendrils that had escaped around her face. The makeup was done dramatically but not in a cheap way. She had plump, pouty red lips that perfectly complemented her red dress, which hugged every curve and had a neckline that scooped down, revealing enough cleavage that made you wish for a bit more. She was elegant and sophisticated. This woman was not me.

"Shit, Andi. You're in the wrong profession," I proclaimed.

"God, you look beautiful. There was no way I was letting you sit in a shitty cab looking like a queen, so I had Jackson send George for you. He'll be here any minute."

"As much as I want to groan and pout, thank you. I am still rattled about the whole Cole thing, so I will feel safer riding with George," I told her.

She smiled knowingly. "All right, toots. Knock 'em dead!"

I walked through the doors into the lobby and my breath hitched. Everything had come together wonderfully. The décor was swanky and classy. Staff members were running around, putting last touches on the tables. Stan wasn't anywhere to be found, so I decided to look for him in his office to see what I should do before the guests arrived.

Stepping into his office, I didn't see him right away. When I realized that he was standing behind the door and buttoning his dress shirt over his muscled chest, I quickly turned away.

"Stan, I'm so sorry. I didn't expect for you to be getting dressed in here," I muttered as I started to leave the office. His hand quickly latched onto my arm, pulling me around to face him.

"Pepper? My God, you look amazing. Woman, where have you been all my life?" he praised, looking over my body, his gaze lingering at my breasts. I could feel my cheeks burning with embarrassment.

"What would you like me to do before the guests arrive?" I questioned, changing the subject.

His eyes darkened as he glanced down at my chest again. With his hand still firmly gripped around my arm, he leaned into me with his mouth at my ear. "I could think of a few things," he whispered, his hot breath tickling my ear.

"Stan, I have a boyfriend. Stop playing around," I stammered, trying to pull my arm from his grasp.

"He doesn't have to know," he growled, sucking my lobe into his mouth.

Turning quickly, I slapped him hard across the cheek. His shocked look was fleeting and then replaced by a scowl.

"Wait by the front and greet guests as they come in," he

snapped as he finished buttoning his shirt.

Without another glance in his direction, I rushed out of his office.

Chapter Thirty

Jordan

AFTER SOME BEGGING, I was finally granted an appointment with Lou and Calvin for tomorrow. The phone call pushed me behind so I had to rush, quickly swinging by the apartment to change into my tux. Andi had already taunted me earlier with a text saying that I was going to "bust a nut" when I saw Elizabeth. That girl was crazy, but I had a feeling she was telling the truth.

Hopping out of the car, I handed over the key to the valet and accepted my ticket. When I walked into the museum, my eyes scanned the growing crowd for my girl. I could care less about the gala. The whole thing was just a way to see her. Now that she was mine, I couldn't wait to take her on my arm and show her off.

Not finding her, I made my way to the auction table. Glancing through the items, I looked for anything that might strike my fancy. When I came across a New Year's Eve romance package that included a stay at the unique hotel at The Standard in The Liberty Suite, I snatched up a pen. The package included VIP access to a Times Square ball drop party with some popular celebrities and musicians. It looked like it would be a blast. I scrawled out an expensive number, hoping I'd win it for us.

I continued perusing the crowd, looking for her. A server offered me a glass of wine and I accepted it.

"Well, the main sponsor of the night finally decided to show up," her familiar voice teased from behind me. After I spun around to see her, my eyes nearly popped out of their sockets.

"Elizabeth, you look gorgeous. That dress was made for your body," I gushed, hugging her to me. She smelled amazing as well.

Leaning forward to her face, I pressed a kiss to her lips. It was a bad idea because then I wanted more than just a simple peck. Feeling the same way, she parted her lips to invite me in, and my tongue greedily tasted her.

"Pepper, I hope you don't greet all the guests like that. We wouldn't want them to think this was a whorehouse," a voice snapped beside us.

Breaking from our kiss, I spun around to see Stan glaring at us. I didn't care if he was her boss. He was about to get an earful.

"Excuse me?" I seethed, giving him a chance to correct his words. Elizabeth grabbed my arm to keep me from throttling him. My body burned with a desire to punch him in the face.

"As much as the museum appreciates Pepper going to great lengths to make our guests feel welcome, she's needed in other areas. Now if you'll excuse me." Stan stalked away while I glowered after him.

"Sorry. That was unprofessional. I really must go work," she stated shakily.

I clasped her hand into mine and brought it to my lips, kissing the top of it. "If you must," I sighed. She nodded and pulled away, heading for a group that had just walked in.

My eyes found Stan again, and he was watching her with a satisfied smirk on his face. That dickhead wanted her. *Over my dead body.*

The evening progressed successfully. Elizabeth was in her element, and the guests seemed to adore her. We spent the entire night apart, stealing glances at each other from afar. It was almost impossible to remain focused on my sponsorship speech since I only wanted to think about and look at her. Thankfully, I kept the speech short in an effort not to embarrass myself.

I was respecting her responsibility for the night, which was difficult since she looked like a damn goddess. Knowing that she was going home on my arm allowed me to control myself from tossing her over my shoulder and taking her to a dark corner. I looked forward to sliding the silky material off of her body later.

As the event came to a close, they announced the auction winners, and I had in fact won the romance package. She grinned at me when she realized I had bid on it.

The museum president, Mr. Callahan, was just thanking everyone for coming when a burning smell permeated the room. Everyone started to look around in an attempt to locate the origin of the smell. From down the hallway rolled a large janitorial linens basket, flames shooting high from inside, licking halfway to the ceiling.

The sight was such a shock that everyone just stared momentarily as it came to a stop in the middle of the room. It was then that I saw Elizabeth bolt for a fire extinguisher on the wall. She almost made it back to the flames before the sprinklers in the ceilings showered water down over everyone near the fire. Running to her, I grabbed the extinguisher from her and proceeded to put out the flames. She and several people started running for some of the priceless exhibits nearby, trying to shield them from the water that was relentlessly cascading over everything in the vicinity.

Guests were screaming and running everywhere, trying to escape the water. Snatching a tablecloth from one of the tables and knocking all of the dishes into the floor, I ran it over to the highlighted exhibit and covered it. Seeing what I had done, several other guests and employees did the same thing in an attempt to shield the paintings and sculptures from the water. Eventually, someone was able to get the sprinklers turned off. The sprinklers were only on for a couple of minutes at the most, but the gala had been ruined.

People walked around, sloshing through water and looking dazed. Mr. Callahan was apologizing to anyone and everyone. The sounds of sirens could be heard over the nervous chatter in the room. When I looked over at Elizabeth, my heart sank. Her hands covered her face and her shoulders heaved. I swiftly made it over to her and hugged her to me.

"He did this, Jordan," she sobbed into my chest. My body tensed at the realization that it most definitely had been Cole. I kissed the top of her wet head and rubbed her back.

"Shh, babe. Everything's going to be okay," I promised. My patience for assholes was wearing thin.

Her body began shivering as the chilly air swept into the room when the firemen walked in. Yanking off my jacket, I wrapped it over her shoulders. It was wet too, but at least it protected her a little.

"Jordan, I don't feel so well. My head is pounding," she whined. I could tell she was close to losing it, so I slid my hand into hers and led her down the hallway to her office.

Once inside, I closed the door and helped her to her chair. Seeing a sweater hanging from her door, I pulled it off and brought it to her. She shrugged out of my wet jacket and let me put the sweater on her.

"Jordan, this is terrible. It's all my fault," she wailed. Her hair was plastered to her head and black mascara streaked her cheeks.

"Babe, you can get over that idea real quick. Nothing about this is your fault. We need to call your dad and tell him though." She nodded but made no moves to get her phone. I opened a few drawers until I found her purse and retrieved her phone.

"Hello Princess, how did the Gala go?" Calvin asked happily.

"Calvin, it's me, Jordan," I informed him.

"Is everything okay with my girl?" he questioned nervously.

"Actually, it's not. We're pretty sure Cole just pulled a big stunt. Someone sent a cart full of burning linens into the main room of the gala. The sprinklers were activated and it ruined the event. Some paintings were probably ruined as well. Thankfully only the sprinklers near the flames were activated."

"Mother fucker," he growled into the phone. I knew he was talking about Cole, and I couldn't agree more.

"He also left her a note on her doorstep this afternoon. The guy won't stop until he's fulfilled his threat. We need to get ahead of him and do something before it gets out of control."

"Shit. Is she going to be okay?" he asked in a worried tone.

"She'll be okay. She is amazingly resilient. We need to catch this asshole. I don't want him messing with my girl any more than you want him messing with your daughter. We have to fix this."

"Thank you, Jordan, for looking after her. I'll call my PI now to see if there's an update and let him know about tonight. Tell her we're going to put him away. I don't want her to worry about him anymore."

"Yes, sir."

Chapter THIRTY -ONE

Elizabeth

FIRST I WAS SHOCKED. Absolutely dumbfounded at the turn of events. My shock quickly morphed into fury. I was livid that Cole was being so vindictive. Luckily, the museum had a high-tech sprinkler system that only activated in the presence of real heat. But even though only a few of the sprinkler heads were triggered, it still caused a lot of damage.

"Babe, are you going to be okay?" Jordan questioned softly. He was watching me with the same face Daddy made when he was worried about me.

"Yes, I'm going to be okay. Jordan, I'm so fucking pissed I can't even see straight."

He walked over to me and enveloped me in a wet embrace.

"I know you are. We're going to figure this out. Cole is psychotic, but I'm sure your dad's PI will find something on the guy."

I nodded my head and pulled away. "Let's go, Jordan. I need to get back out there and help with the cleanup. You can go home if you want, but I need to stay."

"Like hell I'm letting you leave my sight now. Between Cole and that douchebag of a boss you have, you will be safest by my side. Come on. Just tell me what you need for me to do. I know you like to order me around, and secretly, it turns me on," he teased, grinning at me. With a wink, he latched onto my hand and led me back out towards the chaos. Jordan always had a way of making me smile even when I was upset or pissed. He was definitely a keeper.

As we made it back into the main room, firemen were surveying the damage. Stan waved me over when he saw me.

"Pepper, I'm going to go call a fire and water restoration company. Make sure to apologize to any guests still lingering. Mr. Callahan has already spoken to the firemen. It appears that there was an accelerant used in the basket. The police are looking into the janitors we use to see if there is a connection."

"I need to tell you something," I began as Jordan squeezed my hand for support.

"What is it, Pepper?" he clipped out impatiently, clearly wanting to run and make his phone call.

"I think I may know who started the fire, Stan."

"What the hell? What do you mean you may know who started it?" he demanded angrily. Jordan tensed beside me.

"There is a guy who has been threatening me. I actually received another one of his threats today before the gala. It wouldn't hurt for the police to look into him."

"Shit, Pepper! Bringing your damn drama into the museum? Do you know how much fucking damage was caused? Get your ass over there to the policeman and tell him what you know. Shit!"

"Dude, if you yell at her one more time, I'll fucking cause some damage. Not one bit of this was her fault. She is a victim, so leave her the fuck alone," Jordan growled at him.

Stan's face turned bright red and the air was thick with tension as he clenched his jaw, mulling over what Jordan had said.

"Whatever. Pepper, take care of it. We'll talk tomorrow. In the meantime, take it to the police and let's get this shit cleaned up before Mr. Callahan has our asses," he ordered, stalking away.

After a very long night of explaining my theories to the cops and cleaning up the water, we were finally headed back to my apartment. The police were going to question Daddy about his knowledge in regards to Cole. Hopefully they would be able to incriminate him for the fire. The cleanup wasn't too bad. Thankfully, not many of the pieces were really damaged. It was the mess of the food and the dishes all over the floor that we'd spent the most time cleaning up. Had Jordan not thought to cover the pieces with the tablecloths, the damage might have been more extensive.

Walking in the apartment, I noticed a black jacket draped over the recliner. It looked like Bray's. He must have left it yesterday after the party. Everyone had been pretty wasted.

After we made it back to my room, Jordan shut the door behind us and headed straight to the bathroom. I heard the shower turn on before he came back out to me.

"Babe, I think we are more than deserving of a hot shower right about now," he said, peeling off his damp clothes.

"I completely agree, Jordan. Can you help me with my dress?" I asked, turning my back to him.

He came over to me and unzipped the dress but didn't move away. Instead, he slipped his hands into the dress from the back around to my stomach. The chill of his hands caused my breath to hitch.

"You are so beautiful. Even when sopping wet, crying, and with makeup running down your face, you mesmerized me tonight. Everything about you draws me in." He pulled his hands back out and brought them to my shoulders, slipping my dress off. The silky material, no longer wet, slid to the floor in a heap around my ankles. "Damn, woman. Did you pick out those panties and bra just for me?" His hands rubbed down along the sides of my ribs and stopped to cup my ass.

"No, for my other boyfriend," I teased.

He growled at me and nipped my bare flesh where my neck met my shoulder. Laughing, I tilted my head to give him better access.

"I would happily kill any man who ever looked at you, babe. You bring out my inner caveman," he whispered, sucking my neck into his mouth, making me moan. I could feel his arousal hardening up against me from behind.

"Oh God, please don't tell me you're envisioning me barefoot and pregnant in the kitchen. Kill me now," I joked.

"Woman, that is actually a really fucking hot image," he murmured into my ear. Quickly, he spun me around to face him. His eyes skated across my body appreciatively. I thought he was going to kiss me, but he surprised me by heaving me over his shoulder.

"Shit! Jordan, you really are a Neanderthal. You can't keep tossing me over your shoulder. Next thing I know you'll be dragging me around by my hair."

Once he carried me all the way to the bathroom, he finally set me back down. All kidding had subsided, and he stared at me with such intensity that I almost looked away. Reaching around me, he unfastened my bra and slipped it off. His eyes hungrily looked over the swell of my free breasts. Squatting down, he slid my panties down to my ankles, and I stepped out of them. He gently leaned over and kissed the skin between my belly button and pubic bone. My heart rate instantly picked up at the strangely erotic touch.

"Come on, babe," he groaned, standing again, and guided me into the shower with him.

Lathering up the loofa, he began a slow, teasing wash all over my body. Starting at my breasts, he carefully washed each one and in between. When he washed a little lower on my stomach, I started panting as the anticipation grew. As he got near my sex, he avoided it and washed my thighs. I throbbed for his touch on my most sensitive area. After he made his way to my back and ass, I was crazy with need.

"Jordan, I need you right now. You're such a damn tease. I can't wait any longer," I uttered breathlessly.

He chuckled as he ignored my request and washed my hair. While he washed his own hair, I admired his physique. His eyes were closed, his thick, dark lashes resting on his upper cheeks. The five-o' clock shadow along his cheeks and jawline was sexy as hell. His broad shoulders were perfectly sculpted, indicating regular physical workouts. The dark nipples on his chest were standing erect, making me want to put one between my teeth. His abs were flawless and defined. Looking lower, I was mesmerized by the size of his—

"Like what you see?" he asked, interrupting my ogling.

I laughed, embarrassed, but when I looked back up at him, his eyes were burning with need. He quickly reached behind me and turned off the water. I stepped out of the shower to look for a towel, but before I could grab it, he spun me around to face him.

Leaning over, he roughly brought his lips to mine, scratching my chin with his own stubbly one. He sucked my bottom lip in between his teeth and bit down, producing a whimper on my part. Reaching down, I grasped his cock and stroked it while he kissed me.

"Lie down right here," he demanded gruffly. Complying with his request, I stretched out over the cold, tile floor.

"Shit, Jordan, it's cold," I cried out, shivering. We were still wet from having not dried off after our shower.

"You'll be hot in no time," he promised, lowering himself over me.

Without any warning, he shoved his cock into me and I gasped. I was already so wet for him that he slid right in. My legs curled possessively around his hips. As he started pounding into me, my wet body skimmed away from him on the wet tile. As I reached out for anything to keep me still, my hands found purchase on the doorframe and edge of the cabinet.

His hammering into me continued as the sounds of our wet bodies slapping together echoed through the bathroom.

"Jordan, this is so hot. I'm getting close, babe," I moaned and sucked his earlobe into my mouth. My climax was so close. When I felt him finally come inside me, I lost it as my orgasm pulsed around his throbbing length.

His eyes found mine, and they were full of an unexpressed emotion I hadn't seen from him before. I felt that my own gaze matched his. The relief in his eyes made my heart swell, and we both grinned at each other.

We spent the rest of the night trying to express our emotions through our bodies.

Chapter THIRTY-TWO

Jordan

"SO AS YOU CAN SEE, Mr. Jennings, it would be in your best interest to cooperate with us and the SEC," AJ stated, addressing both Lou and Calvin.

Lou grunted, clearly pissed, but Calvin was already nodding his head.

"Lou, they have a point. We need to do what we can to get the proper evidence stacked against Nadia. She's been the big player in this mess, and it's only fair that she takes the fall for it," Calvin told Lou.

"Fine. So I lose a big chunk of money along with countless other investors. What do we do now?" he asked AJ.

"Pete Sands from the SEC is a good friend of mine. He's listing out everything we need to provide to prove Jordan's and Jackson's innocence. I have to contact each and every investor to get information on their involvement. I'm going to advise the investors to avoid any and all contact with Nadia. We're going to close the accounts she's been depositing to and writing checks from. That will stop her little scheme and will probably send her into hiding. Compton Enterprises will do what it can to pay back the original investors, but some of the larger ones will need to be negotiated with to pay back over a series of time. Lou, yours was one of the larger investments, so we're asking you to give them a little extra time to pay you back. Everything from here on out is going to be carefully recorded and calculated to outline a clear and evident trail. Even though there was illegal activity, Compton Enterprises is going to do due diligence to rectify their involvement even when it was done unknowingly in an effort to save their reputation," AJ explained.

"Lou, I'm so sorry about all of this. I don't know how Dad got involved with this, but I'm thinking it had something to do with the fact that he was using the wrong head when it came to judgment. I'm pretty sure Nadia seduced my father so that she could further her own agenda. She's left a path of destruction in her wake, and we need to take the bitch down. I'll get your money back to you, Lou, because my brother and I are men of integrity. It might kill the company in the process, but it must be done," I declared to him.

"Let us know what else we need to do and my client will co-operate. He too is a man of honesty and integrity. Keep us advised on the progress. Jordan, do you think you could speak with me after on an unrelated matter?" Calvin asked.

The other men left the conference room to me and Calvin.

"How's my daughter?" Calvin questioned, getting right to the point.

I hadn't spoken to her much today. She had been busy with the fallout on the museum disaster, and I'd been in over my head dealing with the fraud with AJ all day.

"I shot her a text around lunch. She was flustered about everything, but she's tough. We spoke to the police, and they were going to be contacting you. Have you spoken to your PI?" I asked him.

"Yeah, that's actually what I wanted to talk to you about. He found that Cole's been charged with two counts of aggravated assault from prior altercations with two different women. The problem is that he can't be found. He has his parents' address listed on any formal documentation, but they say he hasn't lived with them in years. It would appear that he is flying under the radar, which is making it a bitch to find him. I'm certain with the findings of the PI, the evidence they uncover from the fire, and Elizabeth's testimony, we have enough for a case against him. The problem will be finding the bastard and keeping my daughter safe in the meantime." His voice was laced with worry.

"Calvin, I would die before I let anything happen to her. She's so damn stubborn though. If it were up to me, I'd have her by my side every hour of every day. You know how she is though. She's independent and strong-willed. I'm thinking of buying us each a handgun and taking her to the range to learn how to use it. If she won't let me protect her, I at least want her to be able to protect herself."

"Jordan, that's a great idea. Sandra and I would like to have you both over for dinner again tonight. I can assure you it will be better than the last time."

"Sir, let me check with Elizabeth, but I think she'd really like that. Six sound okay?" I asked. It was amazing that, in just a couple of days, we went from hating each other to behaving rather civilly.

"Six it is. I'll let Sandra know. See you soon, Jordan," Calvin said, slapping my shoulder as he walked out.

I sent Elizabeth a quick text telling her about dinner plans and then called Jackson.

"Hey, Jordie, what's up?" he asked when he answered the phone.

"Hey, Jackie. So I have some news. Looks like things will get worse before they get better. Now that the SEC is involved and we're closing those accounts, everything is about to come to a head. I just met with Lou. They are going to be patient with us in allowing more time to pay them back. By the time we pay all of those investors their original money, we'll have eaten through most of our capital."

"Well, shit."

"Tell me about it."

"At least I have some good news, Jordie. Nadia finally signed the papers for our divorce. Joel ran it up to the courthouse today. He's going to get it pushed through. At least our divorce will be finalized even in the midst of all of this chaos. She can't stall it anymore."

"That's awesome news. Congrats, man. Oh, by the way, I can't hit the gym tonight because I'm going to dinner with Elizabeth at her parents' house."

"It still throws me off when you call her that. I'm surprised her dad would even want to see you again."

"Jackie, Elizabeth is her name. I think we can all encourage her to go by it. Pepper is the name that fucker gave her. I want to kill him, man. That's something Calvin and I share, so it makes us buds now."

"Okay, dude. Mom called earlier and needs me to help her install her new washing machine. Guess you dodged a bullet there. Again. No worries. Bring her more chocolate and you'll be golden," he teased.

"Ha! Have fun with that," I chuckled and hung up.

"Jordie! So glad to see you again," Sandra gushed as we hugged. "Where's my girl?" she asked, looking behind me.

"She swung by her apartment on the way here to return your

jewelry she borrowed for the gala. She's probably twenty minutes behind me. Dinner smells delicious," I praised, walking into the foyer.

"Oh, hon, you're in for a treat. I've got a crockpot going with my special roast. Calvin usually eats half the pot by himself. I made sure to double my recipe today," she said, smiling.

I followed her into the kitchen and peeked under the lid. "We should eat it now. Just to make sure it's seasoned properly," I advised, pulling out a hot carrot and popping it into my mouth.

"Jordan Compton! Get your hands out of there this instant," she chided, swatting at me. I laughed and took a seat at the bar.

We chatted for a couple of minutes about her church group until Calvin came in through the garage. He walked over and kissed her cheek. Since her back was turned to him, he sneaked over and pulled out a carrot, dropping it into his mouth.

"Dammit, Calvin! You two are impossible. Wait until Elizabeth gets here and keep your fingers out of the food," she admonished, shaking her finger at us. We roared in laughter and she simply shook her head at us.

After a glass of wine and discussing more of the future of my company with Calvin, I glanced over at the clock. Following my gaze, Calvin frowned.

"When was she supposed to get here?" he questioned.

"She should have been here about fifteen minutes ago. I'm going to call her and make sure everything's okay," I told him, pulling out my phone. He nodded, still frowning.

When she didn't pick up, I cursed. Calvin reached down and grabbed his phone, dialing her. The phone went to voicemail again. After dialing her unsuccessfully one more time, I finally dialed Andi. Her phone didn't pick up either. My heart started beating wildly in my chest. When I looked over at Calvin, we both jumped up from the bar and stalked out of the kitchen.

Calvin called over his shoulder, "Sandra, stay here in case she shows up. We're going after her."

Chapter
THIRTY
-THREE

Elizabeth

AFTER AN EXHAUSTING DAY dealing with the after-
math leftover from the gala, I was more than thrilled to be having
dinner with Jordan and my parents. Throughout the entire ordeal,
Daddy and Jordan seemed to have found some common ground. I
knew that if they'd give it a chance they would like each other.

Mom had texted me earlier, informing that we were having her
special roast, and my stomach grumbled just thinking about it. Stan
had been riding everyone's asses so nobody had gotten lunch today.

I had my keys ready when I reached the door to the apartment
and easily unlocked it, going inside. When I went to close the door,
a foot stopped it. Before I even had time to process that, Cole came
pushing through the door, pointing a gun at me. My heart started
pounding loudly in my chest as I attempted to figure out what to
do.

"Well hello, Peppermint Pussy," he said, smiling at me. His
teeth had started to yellow and he reeked of smoke. The hair on his
face hadn't been shaved in what appeared to be days. His once
muscular physique was now flabby.

"What do you want from me?" I demanded, trying to keep the
quiver from my voice. He scowled at me, taking a step forward.

Instinctively, I backed up until I was against the wall.

"I want to finish what I started. You and your father ruined my life. I'd love nothing more than to ruin yours. Time was good to you, Peppermint Pussy. I want to fuck you now more than I did that day. There hasn't been a day gone by that I didn't imagine taking you like I should have long ago."

I glanced down the hallway and saw that my bedroom door was open.

Without a moment's hesitation, I took off in a full sprint towards my room. Seconds later, his heavy footsteps pounded after me. Flying into my room, I slammed the bedroom door shut behind me and turned the lock moments before he flung himself against it.

Fumbling in my coat pocket, I tried to quickly retrieve my phone. My violently shaking fingers desperately searched for Jordan's number. I felt sick when I heard a female's voice on the other side of the door, causing me to pause my search.

"Pepper?" Olive's voice squeaked out from the other side. Shit, he had Olive.

"Don't fucking open the door!" Andi shouted at me. I then heard a scuffle and some crying followed by a thud. My heart tightened in my chest.

"Open the door, Peppermint Pussy, or your girlfriends are going to each take a bullet in the head," he seethed from the other side.

I could hear Olive crying. Quickly, I shot Jordan a text, turned the phone on silent, and tucked it under my pillow. Rushing over to the door, I swung it open.

Cole pointed for Olive to go into the room with me. With his gun still trained on us, he pulled an unconscious Andi by her hair. Olive started crying loudly, and I stepped in front of her to shield her from seeing Andi. Once he got her inside, he shut the door.

"Cole, just let them go. You can have me. Please, just leave them alone," I calmly told him. My attempt to stay calm was shattered when he stalked over to me and put his hand around my throat.

"You don't fucking make the rules!" he roared, tightening his grip.

I gasped for air and frantically tried to claw at his hand to release me, but he was too strong.

"Let her go!" Olive screeched, her tiny frame trying to pull him off of me.

"Bitch, you better back off right now or I'll shoot her!" he spat at her.

Defeated, she stumbled away, sobbing loudly. Releasing my neck, he spun me around and pushed me onto the bed. I frantically sucked in air, momentarily stunned from being choked. When I felt him fumbling for my pants, I weakly attempted to fight him off.

The coolness of the barrel against the back of my neck made me pause in my struggles. My breaths were ragged from lack of air and exertion. Olive continued to wail from her crouched position beside Andi. Cole yanked off my coat.

"You fucking ruined my life, Peppermint Pussy. I had a football career ahead of me and your fucking dad killed it. I'm a fucking loser now because of you and him. When I fuck you, I hope it hurts. And before you can recover, I'm going to do it again. When I've had my fill, I'm going to shoot you in the fucking head."

Anger rushed over me. This asshole just wouldn't go away, and it pissed me off more than it scared me.

"Cole, do you think getting your dick wet is going to change anything here? You'll still be a fucking loser. You are a fucking dog that needs to be put down," I spat angrily. He was going to kill me anyways. Might as well say my piece.

"Bitch!" he screamed and began yanking down my jeans. I squirmed and struggled, landing a kick to his crotch. He stumbled away briefly before he charged back at me, grabbing a handful of my hair.

"You can kill me but you won't get to rape me alive," I panted, still struggling.

Even though he was a lot larger than me, he wasn't as strong as he once had been as a teenager. He flipped me back over onto my back and struck me with the side of the gun, making me immediately see stars.

When I finally blinked them away, I realized he already had my pants halfway pulled down. He no longer had the gun in his hand, so I seized the opportunity to attack him. Sitting up, I shoved both hands into his hair and yanked as hard as I could. Halting his task with my pants, he grabbed my wrists and jerked them away. As he twisted my wrists behind me, I felt my left one snap, sending agonizing pain searing up my arm. I wailed in agony.

The anger faded as tears of pain took over. I stopped my struggle in hopes that he would release my screaming wrist. He let go, laughing at me.

"Maybe I should break the other one too. See how you fight then?" he asked hatefully.

Tears streamed down my face, but I maintained my own furious glare, refusing to let him see me in a weakened state. I would die fighting him off.

Pushing me back down onto my back, he jerked my shirt up to my neck and bit my nipple through my bra. Yelping in surprise, I went to swat at him but pain seared through my wrist again, stopping me.

He continued to pull my pants the rest of the way off. My eyes flitted over to Olive and Andi. I saw Olive quietly pulling her into the bathroom, and the door softly clicked behind them. When two big hands jerked my knees apart, my eyes flew back to Cole. He'd somehow managed to get his pants down as well.

It was over. He was about to rape and kill me. Anger built up again, quelling the fear. Summoning up all of my strength, I pulled my leg from his grasp, kicking him hard in the throat.

"Fuck!" he gasped, stumbling away from me.

I rolled off the bed and away from him, crying out when I landed on the floor with my hands underneath me. Scrambling to my knees, I started to try to bolt from the room when his arms latched around my waist from behind.

I thrashed wildly in his arms as he forced me back over to the bed, throwing me facedown onto the mattress. He was still stronger than I was, but I would still fight while I could.

"Stay fucking still!" he screamed, completely enraged.

Ignoring him, I kept bucking and twisting. Both of his hands found my throat this time. Instantly, I was gasping for breath but still attempting to pull his hands from me, digging my nails into them as hard as I could. The pain in my wrist was excruciating, but I continued to fight madly.

Darkness began eating at the edges of my vision. My lack of air was quickly weakening me. The clawing soon gave way to soft slaps in an attempt for him to release me. Finally, my hands just rested on his when I finally blacked out.

Chapter THIRTY -FOUR

Jordan

CALVIN AND I DROVE in silence on the way to Elizabeth's apartment. We both knew something was wrong. About halfway there, we got stuck behind a fender bender.

"Shit!" I yelled, striking the steering wheel with both fists.

"When we get up here, hang a right. We'll go around," Calvin advised as we inched forward. My phone chimed, indicating a text, and my heart pounded with hope when I saw her face pop up on the screen. After I opened the text, the color drained from my face.

Elizabeth: He's here with a gun. The girls are in danger too. Call 911!

"Fuck! He's got her and the girls!" I shouted, tossing the phone to Calvin.

"Mother fucker!" he roared and quickly used his phone to dial the police. Taking my phone back, I called Jackson.

"Hey, Jordie. Decide you want to come help with this bitch of a washing machine?" he asked with a chuckle when he answered the phone.

"Jackie! Cole's got Elizabeth and the girls. He's at their apartment. Calvin and I are on our way, but we got caught in a fucking traffic jam! Get over there now. The police are on their way too," I rambled quickly.

A slew of curse words spewed from him on the other line. "I'm on my way," he assured me, hanging up.

"Calvin, we're not getting anywhere. I have to get to her. Take the car. I'm going to run up the block and catch a cab past the wreck," I declared, unbuckling my seatbelt.

He leapt out of the car, coming to sit in the driver's side. I was already bolting in a full-on sprint by the time he'd closed the car door.

Running as fast as I could in dress shoes, I soon passed up the wreck, pushing pedestrians out of my way as I flew by. Seeing a man about to step into a cab, I jerked him out of the way and jumped in.

"Hey!" he yelled after me, but I ignored him, slamming the door.

"Drive! It's a matter of life and death!" I commanded to the cab driver.

He nodded and peeled out. Nothing was unusual in New York. When I pulled out several hundred-dollar bills as I shouted out the address, he picked up his speed and swerved in and out of traffic. Minutes later, we pulled up to her building, and I slapped his shoulder in thanks, bounding from the cab.

A couple was going in the building and I pushed past them, bolting up the stairs once inside. Taking them two at a time, I dashed quickly to Elizabeth's floor.

Arriving at her door, which was ajar, I slipped in, trying to take stock of the situation. Realizing that there was nobody in the front room, I raced down the hall to her bedroom. Turning the knob, I cursed when I found that it was locked. Taking a few steps back, I ran back forward and kicked hard near the handle. The wood splintered, and one more kick sent it flinging open.

The sight before me almost caused me to vomit. The man that

had to be Cole had his pants down and was leaning over my Elizabeth with his hands around her throat. She was lifeless, and my heart sank.

Coming out of my dazed state, I charged him. Hooking my arms around his neck, I yanked him away from her. We rolled to the floor and each struggled to get the advantage. I was trying to choke him, but when he elbowed me hard in the ribs, I loosened my grip enough for him pull away. Recovering, I jumped back to my feet and punched him hard in the jaw, sending him stumbling back several feet.

Briefly, I glanced over at Elizabeth, who was still sprawled out, half naked on the bed. Cole began charging me, and I jerked my gaze back to him. When he got close, I popped him in the nose, and blood started gushing fast and thick. Unfazed, he continued to make his way to me. Seeing his dick flopping, I punted him hard between the legs. He howled in pain and dropped to his knees. After I kicked him one more time, this time in the face, he fell backwards.

I rushed over to Elizabeth, putting my fingers at her neck to look for a pulse. She was already bruising along her face, and red marks stretched wickedly across her throat. Her pulse was slow, but at least it was still there.

"Come on, baby. I'm here now. Everything's going to be okay. Wake up for me, baby."

She remained unresponsive. Shaking her, I started to cry.

"Dammit, Elizabeth, wake up. I need you. Please don't leave me. I love you, babe. Do you hear that? I love you so much. Please wake up."

Her eyes twitched and my heart soared. Leaning over to kiss her, I was suddenly ripped away from her by an arm around my neck.

He managed to pin me down and punched me hard in the jaw.

While I was struggling to push him off of me, he hit me again, this time in my eye. I could feel it instantly start to swell shut.

Then a gunshot rang out, and I was temporarily stunned. The smell of gunpowder flooded my senses. Blood began to pool on my chest before something heavy slammed over me.

It was then that I heard the screams. Still trying to make sense of the situation, I felt Cole roll off of me. Looking up with my good eye, I saw Olive pulling him off of me, a gun shaking wildly in her hand. Her eyes were wide and panicked. She'd fucking shot him. I owed that girl a big hug.

Lifting myself up, I grabbed her wrist and gently removed the gun from her hand.

"Olive, are you okay?" I asked soothingly.

She nodded and sat down on her bottom beside Cole. I glanced over at him, shocked to see the bullet hole right in the middle of his forehead. Clearly, someone was a good shot. Patting her shoulder, I jumped up to check on Elizabeth.

She was blinking her eyes slowly, still dazed from being choked nearly to death. Yanking the blanket around her, I covered her bare bottom half and pulled her into my lap. Realizing I was finally there, she began sobbing hysterically. Her voice was ragged as she coughed and cried.

"Shh, baby. I have you now. You're safe now. I love you, baby. I love you so much," I crooned into her ear as I stroked her back.

"Elizabeth! Jordan!" I heard Calvin shout from the living room. When he made it into the room and took stock of the situation, he doubled over as sobs racked his body.

Jackson showed up right behind him and frantically looked around for Andi. From the floor, Olive pointed to the bathroom.

"Olive, come here," I softly called out to her. She was still kneeling on the floor.

She stood and sat beside us on the bed. As I wrapped my free arm around her, the girls cried loudly together as they clutched one another. Minutes later, a dazed Andi wobbled out of the bathroom with Jackson's arms around her. When she saw the girls, she rushed over to them. With Elizabeth sitting down beside me, I stood up so Andi could be with her.

Before I could step away, Elizabeth grabbed my hand. Her eyes seemed as if she wanted to say something. I leaned in close to her, and she whispered softly into my ear.

"I love you, Jordan Compton." She pecked my cheek, and I pulled away, smiling at her.

"Back at you, babe."

Chapter THIRTY -FIVE

Elizabeth

WE SPENT THE REST of Friday night explaining to the cops the entire story and getting several of us looked over at the hospital. Cole was dead. End of story. Andi had a concussion but was fine. Olive was still in shock from shooting Cole but would eventually learn to deal with what happened. Jordan still had a swollen-shut eye and bruised ribs.

As for me, I looked a little worse for wear. I avoided the mirrors, but every time Jordan looked at me, he would cringe, making my heart sink. Purple lines marked the side of my face. I also had a huge bruise on my nipple from Cole's savage bite. There were blue fingerprints all over my arms and legs where he'd roughly grabbed me. My neck looked awful and was a reminder of how close to death I had been had Jordan not arrived at that moment. My wrist was the worst. Both wrists had suffered severe bruising, but my left one was broken. I now sported a lovely pink cast. Unfortunately it had been broken in such a way that the doctor wanted to do surgery on it soon.

Jordan brought me back to his place since I had no desire to go back to my room where Cole had been killed.

"Here. You need to eat this," he instructed, pulling me from my thoughts and setting a bowl down in front of me on the coffee table.

The bowl was steaming, and I knew right away that it was Mom's roast. After he sat next to me with his own bowl, we began to eat.

"She made up all of these to-go containers and delivered them to everyone," he said, chuckling. I smiled as I thought of her trying to take care of my friends.

"How are the girls?" I croaked, my voice still raspy.

"I spoke to Jackson and he said Andi was pretty much back to her normal self. Bray said that Olive is doing well."

"Bray? Why would you ask Bray about Olive?" I asked, confused. The pain meds must have been making me loopy because I couldn't comprehend this.

"Well, let's just say he flipped out once he found out what happened and she wouldn't leave his side after he arrived." I still didn't understand why Bray would be comforting Olive.

We continued to eat silently as I pondered his words. Once we were finished, he put the dishes away and came back into the living room.

"Time for a bath, babe," he said and then scooped me up from the couch.

"Jordan, I'm not helpless. I can walk," I whispered. He ignored me and carried me into the bathroom, setting me down on the counter.

Turning on the water, he left and came back moments later with a plastic sack. Reaching into my hair, he gently pulled out my hair tie. After putting the sack over my cast, he used the tie to keep the sack secured.

The tub was getting full, so he turned it off and removed his clothes, giving me a nice view of his muscled ass. I would never tire of looking at his body. Coming over to me, he ever so gently removed my shirt and then my bra. His eyes darkened angrily when he saw the bruise on my breast, but he quietly continued to undress me. Helping me off the counter, he slid down my jeans and panties and then took off each sock.

"Come on, babe." Holding my unbroken hand, he led me to the tub.

Once we were settled in the bath, I draped my arm on the edge of the tub and leaned into his chest behind me. His arms snaked around me and rested at my belly. We stayed like this for a long time, reflecting on the day.

"Jordan, I can't even begin to imagine how close I was to losing my life today had you not stepped in and intervened," I spoke softly.

He kissed the top of my head and sighed. "Babe, I was scared to death that I was going to be too late. When I saw him bent over you and then saw your lifeless body, I was horrified, thinking I'd already lost you." His thumb gently stroked the skin above my belly button.

"You didn't ask if he raped me or not," I whispered as a shudder coursed through my body.

"All that matters to me is that you're okay. You're alive. I can't live without you," he proclaimed.

A tear rolled down my face. "He didn't. I fought him 'til I couldn't fight anymore, but he didn't get the chance. I just want you to know. I still belong to you," I told him tearfully.

He kissed me again, squeezing me gently. "You'll always be my girl. No matter what he did or didn't get to do to you, it doesn't matter. You're mine, babe. Always," he said.

I started sobbing in relief. The torment and terror that I'd lived with for four and a half years was finally over. Jordan just stroked my tummy and kissed my hair repeatedly until I calmed back down. Once I was just sniffling, he sat up and washed my body and his own. Skipping our hair, he stepped out of the tub and helped me out. Wrapping a towel around me, he kissed me tenderly on the lips before grabbing his own towel.

After we dried off, he helped me into an oversized t-shirt. Careful not to put my weight on my wrist, I sank into his soft bed. Sliding in next to me, he curled his body against mine. Sweeping the hair from my neck, he softly placed kisses all over my neck as if to kiss away every bruise. Finally, I rolled over onto my back and looked into his eyes.

"Make love to me Jordan," I spoke lightly.

"But you're injured. I think we should wait until you're healed," he suggested, not sounding completely convinced.

I bit down on my lip, attempting to suppress any more tears from falling. Quite frankly, I was tired of crying.

"Okay," I agreed, trying to appease him, and turned back on my side. A stupid tear rolled out, wetting the pillow underneath me.

He groaned from behind me. "Fuck that. Come here, babe. I'll be gentle," he promised and I grinned, letting him pull me onto my back.

Sitting up, he delicately lifted up my shirt up over my breasts. He leaned over and placed soft kisses on my bruised nipple before moving over to the uninjured one, sucking it into his mouth. I whimpered because now I really wanted him. Sliding my legs around his hips, I urged him closer. Pulling away from kissing my breasts, he looked into my eyes as he slid himself into me.

"Oh Jordan," I gasped as he filled me to the hilt. We stayed in this position a moment. He was so beautiful and perfect. I loved every single thing about him.

When he grinned at me, I melted like I did every time. Dipping down, he kissed me, soft at first, and then it became a series of hungry sucks and licks. I couldn't seem to get enough of his taste. He began pumping into me with quick thrusts, and I found myself getting close to an orgasm.

"God, Elizabeth, I'm going to come," he moaned into my mouth.

I whimpered as my body started shuddering with my climax, and I felt him immediately pump his own into me. Careful not to hurt me, he rested on his elbows above me.

"I love you. Move in with me. There's no reason for you to have to go back to that room. Too many bad memories. Please, I want you here with me every night," he pleaded.

I tossed around his words in my mind before answering. We loved each other. I could still be an independent woman who loved her man. Who lived with her man.

"Yes, I will move in with you. I love you too."

Chapter
THIRTY
-SIX

Jordan

ALL DAY YESTERDAY, Jackson, Bray, and I had moved Elizabeth's personal belongings to my apartment. Andi and Olive had stayed glued to her side on the sofa, only getting up to make her something to eat, grab a blanket, or help her to the bathroom. Elizabeth hated being doted over, but deep down she'd needed that from her friends after the terrifying event they had gone through together on Friday.

Today, we were keeping it low key at my apartment. I'd rented some movies and we stayed in bed all day. Late in the afternoon, Sandra called Elizabeth to check on her. She and Calvin were going to come by later and bring supper. A knock on the door woke us from a nap and I went to the door to let them in.

"Jordie!" Sandra exclaimed, giving me a huge hug.

"Hi, Sandra. What lovely food did you cook for us today?" I asked, trying to peek in the sack she had in one hand.

"Jordan Compton. Get your hands out of there," she chided and playfully pushed me away, heading into the kitchen.

Calvin walked up to me and pulled me into a hug.

"I can never thank you enough, Jordan. My Elizabeth's lucky to have someone like you," he whispered, his voice catching before he backed away. I nodded and grinned at him.

"I'm the lucky one, sir. She's everything to me."

Blinking back his tears, he smiled back.

"Good, because if you don't take care of my daughter, I'll kill you," he teased, walking into the kitchen.

I followed him in there, noticing that Elizabeth had already snuck into the kitchen and was seated at the table, watching Sandra put food on the plates.

"What do you want to drink, babe?" I asked, kissing her forehead. She smiled at me, the sexy one that made me want to drag her back into the bedroom. I didn't know if she knew the effect she had on me.

"How about a shot of whiskey?" she joked, making Calvin frown at her.

"How about no. Whiskey doesn't mix well with hydrocodone. I'll make you a soda instead," I told her.

Calvin chuckled from behind me. After everyone was seated, we began eating.

"Sandra, you outdo yourself every meal. Are you sweet on me?" I asked, earning a blush from her.

Calvin rolled his eyes, and Elizabeth laughed.

"No, seriously. You need your own cooking show or something. Your food is absolutely delicious. You and my mother would get along fabulously. She's a great cook as well," I confided, which received a smile from Sandra. Elizabeth was beaming at me, and I knew I was earning major brownie points.

"Suck up," she said, sticking her tongue out.

On Monday, I sat in the conference room with Jackson, Joel, AJ, Pete from the SEC, and Trent.

"Okay, Pete. Give it to me straight. What's our next move?" I asked, eager to get a move on things.

"Mr. Compton, after working with AJ, I think we have a solution. I'm glad you brought in your financial planner so we can talk this out all at once," Pete said, passing out a spreadsheet to each of us. "As you can see, I have listed out every single company that has deposited into the fraudulent shell account and how much. Out beside it, you'll see if they made their money back or not. The ones without a figure in that column need to be paid back their original investment. If you can do this before year end, you'll be able to start the new tax year fresh," he explained as we all looked over the sheet.

"Pete," Trent began, "according to this, by the time Compton Enterprises pays out to everyone, the company will be completely wiped out of any operating capital. Without working capital, they will not be able to pay their employees or their bills. Is there any other way around this?"

Pete sighed, and my heart sank.

"Unfortunately, Trent, this is what needs to be done to keep the SEC happy. There will still be lawsuits involved, but at least those will be Compton Enterprises against Nadia Compton. We've got quite the case against her, and she'll be prosecuted to the fullest extent of the law. I hate to have to put your company in a precarious position, but it must be done. Surely you have some personal funds you can inject back into the company?" he asked.

Trent just shook his head, and I frowned. We didn't have nearly enough of what it took to run a large company like ours.

"Trent, don't worry about it. Jackson and I have come to terms that this will most likely dissolve our company. Just help us pay out like we are required to do. We'll pick up the pieces where they fall. I'll call a staff meeting tomorrow and prepare the employees.

As long as I give them warning, they'll find jobs in time. I'll write them all letters of recommendation" I assured him.

"Jordan, your ability to keep a positive attitude amazes me. I'm so sorry for this, buddy," he said sadly. I just nodded at him as my heart ached for the employees who were about to lose their jobs.

"Okay, it's settled. Let's get to work on distributing these funds today," Pete said, pulling out his laptop.

We spent the rest of the day tirelessly going through the list and depleting the company of its funds one wire transfer at a time.

Towards the end of the day, Andi came into the conference room.

"Jordan, Mr. Jennings is on the line for you. He said it was urgent that he talked to you," she said, nervous about interrupting our intense meeting.

"Patch him through." When the phone on the conference room table started ringing, I answered. "Jordan Compton."

"Jordan, it's Lou. I thought you were going to wait to pay out on those funds. The bank just called to tell me the balance had been wired. You said you couldn't afford to send it all," he said in complete wonder.

"Sir, I'm actually in a meeting with the SEC right now and his suggestion was to pay everyone back immediately."

"But, Jordan, where does that leave you?"

"Well, Lou, I'll be honest. We're screwed. I'm going to have a meeting tomorrow with the staff and prepare them for the closure of Compton Enterprises. I've got plenty of great people to send your way if you're looking for support staff," I said, sighing.

"This is bullshit!" Lou growled into the phone.

My thoughts exactly. "Sir, it must be done."

"We're on our way. See you in fifteen minutes," he said, hanging up.

Jackson looked up at me expectantly.

"Looks like Lou is coming up here for some reason," I told him, shrugging my shoulders.

Turning my attention back to Pete, we continued down the list. Fifteen minutes later almost on the dot, a red-faced Lou burst into the conference room with Calvin hot on his heels.

"What's this bullshit?" he demanded to Pete since he was sitting right beside me. Pete glanced at me and I just nodded my approval to tell him.

"Well, sir, we're paying out to all of the investors and unfortunately it will bankrupt this company."

"Unfortunately? That's your word. It fucking sucks," he roared. "All of these employees are about to lose their jobs. Two bright young men are about to have the company they've worked hard to take control of after their father selfishly killed himself yanked out from underneath them. All you can say is 'unfortunately'?" he asked.

Pete sat quietly, sensing that Lou wasn't finished.

"How much?" he asked.

We all glanced at one another, not following where he was going with all of this.

"How much will it take, Jordan, to keep the company afloat? I want to invest," he said simply to me.

"Sir, that's really not necessary. We realize that this is our fate and—" I started to explain but Trent interrupted.

"Five million will get them through the next few months, which will allow them to recover with the new jobs they have on the books. I can invest a million."

I stared at him, completely astonished.

"I'll invest a million," Calvin chimed in behind Lou, and my jaw dropped.

"I've got close to a million in my trust that I'll throw in,"

Jackson said, sitting up in his chair. "You've probably got about the same, right?"

Knowing that I didn't, I rubbed my face in my hands. "Actually, I used most of it for the museum sponsorship and the auction," I sighed, defeated.

"No matter. I'll invest two million," Lou said without hesitation.

I looked up from my hands, amazed at these men willing to do whatever it took to keep this company afloat. Suddenly, I was overcome with emotion and excused myself, hurrying into my office.

Minutes later, Jackson came in and hugged me. Normally, I was the hugger, but he'd always known when I'd needed it the most. Once I composed myself, I pulled away. He nodded, leaving the room, and I followed him back into the conference room.

Pete, Lou, and Trent were huddled over the computer, talking excitedly. It was going to work.

Elizabeth was napping when I slipped into the bedroom. She looked so fragile with her cast peeking out from under the covers. Fluttering her eyes open, she caught me watching her and grinned.

"Come here, you. I missed your sexy face," she said sleepily. She was so incredibly beautiful.

As she sat up in bed, the blanket fell to her hips, revealing her naked body. My cock twitched at the heavenly sight. I strode over to the bed, but she stopped me.

"Don't you dare crawl into this bed unless you're naked and ready to make love to me," she said saucily, eyes still droopy from sleep.

A few seconds later, I was naked and under the covers with

her.

"Someone's happy to see me," she giggled, grabbing onto my cock with her uninjured hand.

"And someone is frisky as hell," I teased, kissing her lips. Grinning, she pushed me onto my back and straddled me.

I could still see the bruises all over her body, but it only signified that my girl was a survivor. When she glided herself over my cock, her pussy clenching around it, I groaned in pleasure.

The sight of her head tossed back, breasts bouncing, ensured that I was going to come fast. Helping her along, I stroked her clit with my thumb quickly in a circular pattern—just the way she liked it. Her breathing picked up, and her pants soon turned into moans.

When she clamped down around my cock with her constricting sex, indicating her orgasm, my own release pumped furiously into her, not far behind.

Stretching out over me, she cuddled into my chest. I fought back a wince because of my still aching ribs and clutched her to me. Any amount of pain was worth having her with me like this in this moment. She was perfect and belonged only to me.

As if we'd rehearsed it, we both said in unison, "I love you." She burst into giggles making me slap her on the bottom. Elizabeth grew quiet again as she felt my dick, which was still inside of her, begin to harden. Flipping her over onto her back, I showed her the rest of the night just how much I really did love her.

Epilogue

Elizabeth

New Year's Eve

"I CAN'T BELIEVE how nice our hotel room is!" I exclaimed for probably the hundredth time as we were waiting for the ball to drop. The room was beautiful and had the most amazing bathtub with a gorgeous view of the city. We were half tempted to christen it but needed to get on to the pre-party.

Jordan had paid a lot of money for this package, and it was totally worth it. We'd already gotten to see several performers and even met a few celebrities. The rooftop party had an open bar and was catered with delicious cuisines from an upscale restaurant nearby.

I sighed happily as I thought about how wonderful things had been since I'd moved in with him. My parents adored him. His mother and mine had become quite close over Christmas. Daddy treated him like a son, and they had regular "man dates" at the cigar lounge.

Things were going great with Compton Enterprises as well. As it turned out, Bray was actually pretty useful for something in his life and was nailing business deals faster than they could keep up. I hated to admit it, but he'd actually turned out to be a good friend to the guys. The investors had stayed on, but their funding hadn't been absolutely necessary.

As for Nadia, the bitch had gone down. The case had gone pretty quickly, considering they'd had so much stacked against her. Since Daddy knew the judge really well, she hadn't had much of a chance anyway. She was going to prison for quite a while. Everyone had been completely happy about that revelation. She'd been required to pay restitution to Compton Enterprises for their loss, but they would probably never see a dime of that money. Not that they needed it.

Jordan pulled me out of my daydreaming when he pecked me on the lips.

"Really, babe? I don't think you mentioned it," he teased at my mention of the lovely hotel room once again, causing me to playfully punch him in the gut. "You're so hot when you're violent," he growled, nibbling my ear.

"Gross! You're such a man," I joked but let him pull me into a deep kiss. I'd loved every minute we got to spend together since the day I met him.

"Look, they're about to start the countdown in about a minute," he said to me, pointing at the screen that was counting down.

Giggling, I hopped up and down, overcome with excitement.

"Elizabeth," he said, bringing my face to see his. "You are everything to me. I can't imagine living my life one second without you. We were made to be together. You are the most beautiful woman I've ever laid eyes on. Every day, you amaze me with how funny, intelligent, and strong-willed you are. I love you more than you'll ever know." My eyes grew teary at his sweet words. "I want to see your belly swell one day with the growth of my child. Everything I do, I want you to be a part of it. You're mine, babe. Forever."

When he crouched down on one knee, I gasped, completely at a loss for words. The countdown began. *10, 9, 8...*

"Will you marry me, sweet Elizabeth?" he asked, slipping a gorgeous ring on my now healed left hand. *5, 4, 3...*

"Yes!" I exclaimed, pulling him up to me.

The crowd went wild with one big, "Happy New Year!" and I couldn't help but think that they were celebrating for us. Jordan's mouth captured mine and I shared the most romantic kiss to date with my future husband. *My love.*

The End

Coming Soon...

Scarred (Breaking the Rules #3) – Coming April 2014

Rock Country – Southern Seduction box set novella – Coming April 2014

Moth to a Flame, a novel – Coming May 2014

Apartment 2B, a novel – Coming June 2014

Acknowledgements

Everyone has someone they look up to—a mentor of sorts. That person, throughout this entire process for me, has been Ella Fox. Thank you Ella for always being there for my unending questions, for knocking sense into me when I get too close to the ledge, and for being my friend. Never could I have imagined a year ago when I was reading that adorable Hart family and gushing over the author that wrote them, would I later become good friends with her. You are rad, girlfriend!

I also want to thank my beta readers, whom are also my friends. Holly Sparks, Leann Jester, Mandy Abel, Star Price, and Erica Thompson, you guys provided AMAZING support and feedback. Pointing out areas that didn't work and gushing over parts you loved, you helped boost the confidence I needed to finish what I'd started. I can't thank you enough and look forward to sending you more of my stories in the future.

I most certainly wouldn't be where I was without the love and support of my fellow Indie Romance Author Chicks. You ladies gave me advice when I needed it most and were there when I needed to vent. Without your guidance every step of the way, I'd surely be lost in sea of confusion. Each and every one of you rock. I can't wait to hug all of your necks (even though hugging is totally not my thing) and even put Tessa Teevan in my back pocket because she's so damn cute.

Mickey, my fabulous editor from I'm a Book Shark, without you, my story would have been a mess of overused words. You kept my story consistent with the first book, gently reminding me of what *really* happened. I'm sure you were ready to *pull* your hair out or *grab* your laptop and throw it out the window by the end. My favorite comment was, "Let's give this word a break." Thank you for leaving me happy little smiley faces to soften the blow of my "special" writer moments. My books would be a grammatical mess without you.

Wendy Shatwell and Claire Allmendinger of Bare Naked Words, thanks for pimping my book and holding my hand all the way from the UK. You two really go above and beyond with everything you do—and have incredible work ethic. I can't wait to see what the future holds for Bare Naked Words! Thank you Stacey Blake for formatting my books and making them look gorgeous. You've got talent, kid.

A huge thanks goes out to my wonderful husband, Matt. Without you, I wouldn't have been able to make this dream possible as it took a lot of time and money. Not only did you write check after check when I "needed" something else for my book, but you also kept the children fed and bathed. Tighten those apron straps because I don't have plans of stopping any time soon!

Lastly, but certainly not least of all, thank you to the wonderful readers out there that are willing to hear my story and enjoy my characters like I do. It means the world to me! My heart swells happily every time a reader messages me to tell me how much they enjoyed my book and read it in one night. You guys are fab— cyber kisses and hugs to you all!

About the Author

I'm a thirty two year old self-proclaimed book nerd. Married to my husband for nearly eleven years, we enjoy spending time with our two lovely children. Writing is a newly acquired fun hobby for me. In the past, I've enjoyed the role as a reader. However, recently, I have learned I absolutely love taking on the creative role as the writer. Something about determining how the story will play out intrigues me to no end. My husband claims that it's because I like to control things—in a way he's right!

By day, I run around from appointment to appointment wearing many hats including, mom, wife, part-time graphic designer, blogger, networker, social media stalker, student, business owner, and book boyfriend hunter (It's actually a thing—complete with pink camo. I lurk around the internet "researching" pictures of hot guys that fit the profile of whatever book boyfriend I'm reading or writing about).

I guess you can blame my obsession with books on my lovely grandmother whom is quite possibly my favorite person on the planet. At an early age, she took me to the Half-Priced bookstore each weekend and allowed me to choose a book. Every single time, she caved when I begged for two. Without her encouragement, I wouldn't have been able to cope during some hard times without my beloved books.

Currently, I am finishing up my college degree that has taken me forever to complete. It's just on the list of my many "bucket-list" goals that I subject myself to.

Most days, you can find me firmly planted in front of my computer. It's my life. If the world ever loses power, I'd be one of the first to die—of boredom! But, I guess as long as I have books and a light, I might just survive.

Looking forward, you can expect to see one more novel in the Breaking the Rules Series. Also, I have two standalone novels and a novella that will be released soon as well.

This writing experience has been a blast and I've met some really fabulous people along the way. I hope my readers enjoy reading my stories as much as I do writing them. I look forward to connecting with you all!

https://www.facebook.com/authorkwebster

http://authorkwebster.wordpress.com/

https://twitter.com/KristiWebster

kristi@authorwebster.com

https://www.goodreads.com/user/show/10439773-k-webster

http://instagram.com/kristiwebster

Check out these excerpts from some other really amazing authors…..

Push the Envelope
By: Rochelle Paige

Prologue

Flowers…check.

Chocolates…check.

Champagne chilled and ready to go…check.

Noise-canceling headphones so I didn't have to listen to what-ever noises were going to float up from the rear cabin…check.

This was so totally not the normal pilot's checklist. When I talked to Dad over the summer about offering Mile High Club charter flights so we had some extra money coming in to cover my room and board at college, I had no idea how the idea would take off. I'd figured I would take a couple flights out each month so Dad wouldn't have to scrimp on anything so that I could live on campus. He really wanted me to get the whole college experience, especially since I had chosen to stay in town for school.

Who knew there were so many middle-aged housewives look-ing to spice up their marriages? I usually had three to four flights booked each week now. At a cool grand per booking, we made enough to cover my room and board and maintenance on the planes, and we even had money left over to pay off my student loans and to cover my tuition for my next two years. I guess they're right when the say sex sells!

Since the flights were offered in the evening, they didn't inter-fere with my classes. Dad wanted as little to do with this venture as possible. He had told me that this was my idea, and he expected me to run with it. Talking about anything connected to sex with his daughter wasn't really high on his list of things to do. I figured I was lucky that he was willing to let me use the Cherokee for the flights. I just had to make sure I booked them when I was able to be in the pilot's seat. The last thing I wanted to do was screw my grade point average over because I was skipping too many classes to pilot the flights I was only offering so I could pay for school in the first place.

Today's flight was due to depart in about thirty minutes, so the lucky couple should be here any minute now. I needed to get my butt in gear so I would be ready when they arrived. The plane was set up for their romantic rendezvous. I was dressed in my charter pilot gear of loose khaki pants and a Hewett Charters polo shirt. I'd pulled my long brown hair back in a low ponytail. This appearance seemed to help the wives feel more comfortable with the idea that their pilot was a twenty year-old girl. Add into the equation that I am passably attractive and I could have a problem on my hands with my paying customers. So I did what I could to make sure I presented myself as a capable pilot and nothing else.

I know it's crazy for some people to picture me piloting a plane, but I started flying with my dad before I ever got behind the wheel of a car. He lived to fly and taught me to love it as well. I had my permit when I was sixteen, earned my private license when I was seventeen, and got my professional license when I turned eighteen. Some days it felt like I spent more time during my life up in the air than I did on the ground.

Yet another reason Dad wanted me to live on campus this year—so I could hang out with girls and act my age. Dad and I had been two peas in a pod forever, and now he worried that I needed to have a normal life with girlfriends, parties, and boys. I admit that my upbringing wasn't exactly orthodox, but I was happy with the way things were. I just wished Dad would understand that.

Damn, it sounded to me like my housewife of the day had gone all out for this trip based on the click of her stilettos hitting the tarmac. I didn't understand how women could walk on shoes that looked like skyscrapers to me. Guess that was just the tomboy in me, much to my best friend's dismay. Time to get my head in the game so I didn't scare off the paying customers.

"Welcome to Hewett Charters," I greeted the middle-aged couple as they made their way towards me. "You must be Mr. and Mrs. Williams?"

"Yes, that's us," tittered the platinum-blond woman as her husband looked at me quizzically. I guessed that she hadn't used their real name in the hope that they could keep their trip private. She needn't have had that concern since I offered complete confidentiality.

"Thank you for booking your flight with us today," I said. "Everything is all set, and we can be in flight as soon as you are ready to go. Did you have any questions before we board?"

"Ummmm, are you our pilot?" asked Mr. Williams.

"Yes, I'm Alexa Hewett. Don't worry. You're safe with me. I've been doing private sightseeing tours for a couple years and have had my pilot's license for almost three years. I might be a little young, but I grew up with my dad in the cockpit of a plane. I can assure you that I am fully qualified to take you up," I answered.

"And how does this work exactly?" he questioned.

I couldn't help but smile at the question. It seemed that the wives always booked these flights, and the husbands always seemed uncertain once they got here. I even had flights where the husband had no idea that his wife had booked the tour with the sole purpose of getting it on mid-flight. The expressions on their faces when they saw the bed in the cabin were priceless. It kind of cracked me up since I always figured guys were less shy about sex. Which may still prove to be true since I hadn't seen a single guy yet turn down the opportunity offered by my special charter flights.

"If you will follow me this way, you can see how we've set

the Cherokee up so that you will have plenty of room in the rear cabin. Once we are in flight, I will draw the privacy curtain and wear noise-canceling headphones during the flight. I will be able to communicate with the tower but won't be able to hear anything from the cabin. Any of your activities while on board will be as private as possible." They both nodded and looked at each other while blushing.

I walked the couple towards the plane, showed them the bed area we had fashioned by removing four of the seats, and asked them to sit in the rear-facing seats during takeoff for their safety. If the hot looks they were flashing each other as they buckled up were any indication, they were ready to go.

"Enjoy the refreshments, and I will let you know when it is safe to move about the cabin," I said as I got settled into the cockpit.

As I prepared for takeoff, I couldn't help but chuckle to myself about the irony of me helping couples to spice up their sex lives. I wasn't exactly qualified to do so except for piloting the plane. I couldn't really be described as very experienced in the bedroom. Yet, I have turned my beloved Cherokee into the equivalent of a by-the-hour hotel room.

At Death It Begins
By: Elle Jefferson

Prologue

There was too much noise making it impossible to focus. The clock ticking from an adjoining room, the wooden chair creaking every time he moved, and the sound of her foot tap, tap, tapping beneath the table were crumbling the delicate twine of his sanity. He loosened his tie using the front flap to brush away the sweat gathered along his brow.

She watched him watching her.

The thought of death, especially hers, at his hand sent waves of pleasure coursing through him quieting the hatred spewing in his mind over her misdeeds. Her eyes drifted from him to the back door. That door stood only a yard from her, but her age pitted against his strength—no doubt who'd win.

His gaze, however, fixated on the pendant—an inverted triangle with an inner cross connecting the three sides—twisting on a gold chain around her neck. The edges of the triangle kept catching in the sun lulling him. He glanced at the tattoo on his left wrist. *A perfect match.* How dare this treacherous woman wear such a treasured insignia. *Blasphemous.* His hand contracted into a fist. His breathing drew sharp, *not yet.*

He placed the underside of his wrist facing up on the table exposing his tattoo. Her gaze drifted from his face to his tattoo. She closed her exquisite amber colored eyes. He couldn't keep the grin from his face.

She understood. Only one would be leaving this kitchen.

Whistling pierced the air and he drew his hands to his ears. His gaze followed hers to the stove. He couldn't handle the whistling, the roar piercing the sanctuary of his thoughts.

"May I finish my tea you interrupted?"

He nodded, and with a bit of effort she got out of her chair and hobbled over to the stove. The noise was scattering his thoughts and he growled, "Hurry up!"

"Care for a cup?" She asked turning back to face him.

He did not respond just gave a guttural growl.

She retook her seat eyeing him. "Do I at least get your name? Seems only fair."

"It's inconsequential—" he cleared his throat, "—as am I."

He leaned closer the stench of bourbon and cigarettes ripe on his tongue, "Where are they?"

She recoiled adding precious space between them, "Who?"

He scowled. "Difficulty will get you nowhere." He retrieved a syringe from within the folds of his jacket. A yellow liquid spurted out when he flicked the vial with a finger. "One more chance, where are they?"

"Who?" A tear rolled down her cheek.

"You should think about sparing yourself the pain." Though in earnest, he wanted her to be disobedient. It would make punishing her more satisfying, give a release to his building erection.

She glanced his tattoo, took a shaky breath and narrowed her eyes, "No."

"I hoped you'd say that."

"God is not on your side in this," she said—her final defiance.

Before she could react, he plunged the tip of the syringe into her shoulder.

The lustrous yellow liquid disappeared into her arm. Her heart thumped faster, irregular.

"If He isn't, then perchance you may hazard a reason as to how I found you?"

She tried to retort, but her words froze in her throat. She tried to move, to fight, but nothing responded except her eyes. Her body contorted before seizing up. Unable to catch herself from falling she collided with the floor.

He crouched beside her unable to keep the glee from his voice, "Digitalis is a powerful drug. It's especially potent when mixed with Oleandrin. The toxin renders its victim immobile as it works its way through the blood stream. It can take hours, days even, before causing your heart to explode."

He picked up her head and placed a kiss to her forehead and looked into her eyes, "I will find them." He let go of her head and it hit the floor with a clunk. "You do not deserve this," he said and snatched the pendant from her neck. He tucked the necklace and syringe back in his coat and chuckled as he made his way to the door. He stole one last look at her frozen body on the floor. "They will pay," he said and shut the door behind him.

Goodbye Caution
By: Jacquelyn Ayres

Prologue

December 26, 2012

Dear Journal,

You were given to me today with an encouraging gesture to write my memories down. The task, though it needs to be done, is daunting. My head is spinning. Where do I start?

You see, I've been "lost" for seven years. However, it only took three months and an extraordinary man to find me. I know . . . the math doesn't seem to add up. But it does—you'll see.

I guess the best place for me to start is at the beginning (of the last three months, that is). Everything will fall into place for you from there, just as it did for me. I will write it as I remember it. I don't want to leave a single detail out.

I must warn you (eye roll—only I would warn a journal!) that everything moves along rather quickly. I thought it was odd when it was happening—I couldn't slow things down, let alone stop them. Believe me—I tried! I know . . . I'm rambling. The point is, everything does happen for a reason. They were right! Whomever "they" are. *Shrugs*

And now, without further ado, I give you the story of how this lost woman was found.

*Cue dramatic theatre music (I'm thinking Andrew Lloyd Webber–esque)!

Always,

Becca Campbell

CPSIA information can be obtained at www.ICGtesting.com
Printed in the USA
LVOW11s0512281114

415859LV00010B/444/P